LVING
THE
BLACKSMITH

VIRGINIE
MARCONATO

OLIVERHEBERBOOKS

Loving the Blacksmith Copyright 2025 © Virginie Marconato

Cover art by Dar Albert at Wicked Smart Designs

Published by Oliver-Heber Books

0 9 8 7 6 5 4 3 2 1

PROLOGUE

"Here. It's not much but—"

"It's perfect, thank you."

Agnes looked at the man looming over her, making the room appear smaller than it was. Blond, muscular, with long, flowing hair and eyes as blue as the deepest part of the ocean—the part where she imagined dangerous creatures lurked—he was too perfect to be true. She had thought Björn, the Norseman who'd come to visit Birgit at the village, magnificent enough, but this one was even more compelling. She judged him to be a decade older than Björn and herself, and the added maturity suited his masculine features to perfection. In him, everything was... *more*, somehow. His stance was more assured, his body more developed, his gaze more piercing.

Though he was a stranger, and impossibly large, she felt at ease with him. Perhaps it was the way he had immediately offered her a place to sleep, perhaps it was the way he spoke, with the faintest trace of an accent, perhaps...

Perhaps it was simply the way he looked.

No matter what, she just couldn't get past the attraction she felt. The men in her village had never stirred half the emotions this one stirred in her and she wondered if she should not ask to sleep somewhere else. But where? She only knew Björn and Dunne, with whom she had spent the last few days traveling, and neither had offered to have her.

No, the blacksmith had been kind to offer her a place to sleep, she could not offend him now by asking to go somewhere else. She would simply have to pull herself together and stop gawping at him.

"I use this room to keep old tools," Magnus was saying, mercifully oblivious to her musings. "But it's clean because my brother visits regularly and sleeps in it when he does."

"It's perfect," she repeated. At least she would be alone, and able to decide what to do next. The Norsemen village could only be a temporary stop. As a Saxon, she didn't belong here. But she couldn't go back to her village, knowing what was waiting for her there.

A husband she didn't want.

A life she feared.

Magnus walked over to the pallet. "I'll go and give the furs a shake outside and find a softer blanket for you. This one won't do. Your skin is bound to be more delicate than Sven's." The way he said that, and then cleared his throat, told her the comment had put wholly unsuitable ideas in his mind. Was he imagining her naked and sprawled on the furs for him to gaze upon? Was he thinking of stroking her all over to ascertain just how soft she was? His hands, used to handle the tools around her, would be strong and callused, all the better to awaken her senses.

Heat bloomed under her skin, which suddenly felt as delicate as he'd called it.

"Really, please," she mumbled. "This blanket will do very nicely. I don't want to put you out."

"You're not putting me out."

He bundled the furs up into a ball he lifted as easily as if it had not weighed almost as much as she did. Inexplicably, the sight caused her stomach to flip. Why was the man's strength so appealing? It should have worried her. But for a reason she couldn't explain, it thrilled her.

When he came back a moment later with a soft woolen blanket, she had herself under control once more. The reaction had been as brief as it had been inexplicable. Compelling as he was, the blacksmith was only a man. There was no reason she wouldn't be able to keep him out of her mind, just like she had the others.

She nodded her thanks and watched him walk out of the room.

No. No reason at all.

CHAPTER ONE

Magnus woke up early, as per usual, and went to the chicken coop in search of eggs with which to break his fast. He had spent an agitated night, thinking about the woman sleeping in the room at the back of the forge, with her beautiful green eyes and luminous skin. Her skin that was more delicate than that of his oaf of a brother. Really, what had possessed him to say such a silly thing? Moments after meeting Agnes, he had established himself as an idiot who had no notion how to talk to women, not the impression he wanted to give.

When Björn had come back from accompanying Dunne to Mercia, he had brought with him another Saxon to the village. The poor girl, who, his friend had informed him discreetly, was fleeing a life she didn't desire, needed a place to stay. It had taken no more than two heartbeats for Magnus to know he could not bear having anyone else offer to shelter her.

Why that was, however, he wasn't sure.

She was a tiny, timid thing, who had looked at him in awe mingled with apprehension, not a reaction he was entirely comfortable with. He'd always been attracted to confident women who did not let his stature impress them. He knew he was taller than most men in the village, and days spent hammering in the forge ensured he had developed muscles that rivaled even those of Wolf, the village leader. For that reason, he tended to choose lovers who were on the voluptuous, and assertive side. With them, there was no danger of a mishap. They were strong enough, physically and mentally, to deal with him.

But the problem was, the women he usually favored didn't favor him. And them being brazen ended up causing him more trouble than they were worth. Edith came to mind. As to confidence, surely it had nothing to do with size, and a woman who only reached up to his shoulder and yet was brave enough to stare at him in the eye could teach him a thing or two about it. Perhaps he'd been put in the path of the kind of person he needed rather than the sort he thought he wanted. It was worth pondering about at least.

He was finishing his eggs when a voice cut through his musings.

"Magnus, I knew you would be up. Do you have a hammer I could borrow?" Wolf walked in through the open door, a smile on his face. "I want to start repairing the fence around the vegetable patch and orchard and mine is too small."

"Yes. I have what you need at the forge. Let me get it for you now."

The interruption was welcome. He'd spent more than enough time daydreaming about the little Saxon's soft skin and beguiling ways. It was time to get on with his day.

Quietly, so as not to waken Agnes, he pushed the door of the forge open and walked over to the tool bench. Just as he grabbed the hammer he was looking for, the door to the back room opened—on a surprised, stark naked Agnes.

Everything rushed south at the same time. His heart plummeted to his boots, his blood raced to his groin, his hands fell to his sides and the hammer dropped to the floor, missing his feet by inches.

Magnus stared at the woman revealed in front of him.

He couldn't help it, he didn't even try to stop himself. She was too beautiful. He allowed his gaze to roam over her greedily, taking in every glorious inch before fastening on her breasts. Her perfect, round little breasts topped with rosy pink nipples. His throat went dry at the same time as his mouth started salivating. Had he ever seen anything more arousing than her lithe body? No, he had not. The fact that he'd had no warning whatsoever that she was about to walk into the room only made the sight more shocking. Usually, when he saw a woman's breasts, it was because she was already in his arms, already under him, it was because he'd already made up his mind to have her, and made sure to feast his eyes on her beforehand.

This was nothing like that. He'd been afforded a glimpse of a woman who had not agreed to bare herself to him and the forbidden element added an undeniable thrill to the moment.

He cleared his throat as he placed his hands in front of his crotch. After the way he'd stared at her, the last thing he needed was frighten her with the proof that the sight of her nudity had turned him into a randy stallion ready to cover a mare.

"What in Odin's name are you—"

As soon as he spoke, the spell was broken. Agnes shrieked and disappeared back into the room, slamming the door behind her.

It was only then that Magnus saw the gown and shift

she had draped by the fire embers to dry overnight. How had he missed them? If he'd seen them, he might have guessed she was naked in the other room and made some noise so as to warn her she was not alone. It would have been a pity though. He regretted shocking her, but he could not regret having seen her. Never had he seen a more graceful, enticing woman. He'd noticed she was pretty when she'd arrived, of course, and on the slender side, but he'd never guessed that once she was naked, her lean body would be so compelling.

"Magnus, are you still here?" The voice was hesitant.

He picked the hammer from the floor before answering. Yes, he was still here, still hard, still stunned. "Yes."

"I'm sorry, I know this is your forge, but I need you to leave, so I can get dressed. My clothes are in the other room, you see." She sounded slightly breathless, and he hoped panic was not the cause. He would hate for her to be wary of what he would do now that he had seen her naked. She had nothing to fear, he had no intention of pouncing on her, even if a certain part of his body urged him to do just that. "I washed them last night."

He walked over to the forge to retrieve the pale blue linen dress and impossibly small shift she had placed on the stool. They looked almost like children's clothing and a smile tugged at his lips at the thought. There was nothing childish in the body he had seen. Slender as she was, Agnes was all woman. Thus far, only buxom women with generous hips had stirred his blood. Right now he could think of nothing more arousing than the tight little breasts and lean hips he'd just seen.

"Your clothes are still damp, I'm afraid," he told her, after having ascertained the fact.

A silence. "Oh." Now Agnes sounded dejected. Good. At least she was not afraid anymore.

"I will go and get you one of my undershirts. It will keep you warm while I go and see if someone in the village has a dress I could borrow for you. Ingrid might do."

His first thought had been to ask Wolf's wife, Merewen, whom he knew better than most, but any dress of hers would have swamped Agnes and he didn't want her to feel uncomfortable—or rather, more uncomfortable than she already was.

"Thank you. I don't mean to be such an imposition."

"You're not."

She was anything but. Impositions didn't look anything like her. They didn't make him hard. They didn't have creamy skin, pert breasts, pink nipples and slim legs. It was impossible not to imagine how that skin would warm under his touch, how those breasts would fit in his hands, how those nipples would feel in his mouth, how those legs would wrap around his waist while he—

"Are you still here?"

Damnation, yes, he was, and with an erection to rival the hammer he was holding in his clenched fist both in length and in strength. This wouldn't do. He would have to wait a moment outside the forge before he went hunting for a dress for her. He could not go call on Ingrid in such a state. The poor woman would only take fright.

"Yes. I was only taking some tools I need," he lied. "I'll go get the shirt now."

As SHE SLIPPED the oversized shirt over her head, Agnes tried very hard to ignore the scent of it.

Smoky, yet fresh, as if it had been dried outside, masculine yet sweet, as if it had been spread in a flower-strewn meadow. It was Magnus' scent, as enticing as he was. Everything here was his. It was his shirt, his forge, his life she had disrupted. She now was part of his world, whether she wanted it or not.

And this world was as different as the one she had left behind as night was from day.

Here, she was not insignificant, the daughter of a

man who despised her, but a woman in her own right, and beautiful with it. Magnus certainly seemed to think so. His gaze had been as hot as the coals burning in his furnace when he had walked in on her naked earlier and looked his fill. No man had ever looked at her like that before. No man had seen her naked before. No man had made her want to throw herself into his arms. Everything about this was new, unsettling, potentially dangerous.

Not that she feared Magnus, but herself.

Knowing she could not afford to catch their attention, much less stir their desire, she had always avoided men's company. It was the safest way to act, because the day she gave one the impression she would welcome his advances, all would be lost. He would pounce and she would be powerless to defend herself. She had seen and heard enough of men to know they were ruled by their physical urges, urges that could only put her in danger.

Agnes wrapped the soft shirt around her. It was so big it engulfed her twice over but still it was not enough to chase the chill spreading through her at the thought of a man taking her to bed.

It was not the possession she feared, even if she'd heard the first time could hurt, it was the consequences. Humiliation if her lover abandoned her after having had what he'd wanted from her, marriage if he wanted more of her. In other words, a lifetime of misery, children.

Death.

Her parents' marriage had not been a happy one and had made her dread the same fate. Her mother had found herself constantly with child, or nursing a babe. She had died at a relatively young age, exhausted by the strain put on her body. In her short life, she had borne ten children, three of which she'd had to bury within a week of their birth. Her husband, Orvyn, had never loved nor cared for her, he'd only seen women as bodies to rut on when the need took him. He had not stopped to wonder whether her mother wanted him in her bed mere days after giving birth, or worried about the consequences for her health if she got with child every year. It had been a miserable life, one Agnes had sworn she would not have.

But then she had been told that her father had found her a husband, an old man who only wanted her for the pleasure her young body would offer him in his late life. The thought was horrifying.

That was why when Björn, the Norseman who'd come to visit Brigit, had offered her the chance to leave the village and travel south with him, she'd agreed without hesitation. She did not regret having done so, even if she had left all she knew behind. Here, with no father to pressure her into anything, no old man lusting after her, she would be free to live the life she wanted. The only girl in the family, and the youngest of the surviving children, Agnes had heard all her life that women were only good for two things, slaking a man's lust whenever he wanted relief and bearing the children that inevitably followed, and this without complaint.

Well, she had the audacity to think otherwise.

"Agnes? Are you here? I have a dress for you."

Magnus' voice broke through her grim musings, as welcome as a beam of sunlight in a dark tunnel.

"Yes. Come in."

It was only when Magnus' gaze fastened on her with the intent of a hawk's that she realized she should have asked him to leave the dress in the other room for her to retrieve when she was alone. She also understood from the tightening in his jaw that the shirt, oversized as it was, did little to hide her neck and throat. The collar hung so low on her that it left part of her bosom exposed. The blue in Magnus' eyes swirled and his body tensed, proving he was every inch the hot-blooded male he appeared to be.

And yet, to her surprise and relief, he made no move toward her. He didn't even look his fill, like he had earlier, when he'd seen her naked. After the initial shock, he lowered his gaze to the floor, as if he felt at fault for staring at her. A most unexpected reaction in so virile a man, and endearing.

Her shoulders relaxed and she understood why she had felt at ease with him from the beginning. Here was a man who would not take advantage of her. He might desire her, think her beautiful even, but he would never overstep the mark. Whatever he took from her, she would give freely.

"Here you are. A dress and a shift that will fit you much better than my shirt." Eyes still on the ground, he handed her a soft woolen dress and a plain, serviceable shift. "I asked Ingrid for some clothes. She's the same build as you, I would say, so everything should fit you fine."

Agnes felt herself flush at this reminder of why he could claim to know her size. Had he seen this Ingrid naked, too, she wondered, to be able to compare the two of them thus? Was she his sweetheart? Was that why he had gone to her to borrow the dress? Did he love her? And what difference did it made if he did?

The unwelcome questions assaulted her all at once but she could not ask any of them out loud.

"Ingrid?" was all she said. She had no idea who the woman was.

"She's Björn's sister," Magnus explained rubbing the back of his neck. He knew that, apart from Dunne, Björn was the only person she knew from the village so it stood to reason he would use him to make her see who Ingrid was. But this answer did not satisfy her. What she really wanted to know was, what was Ingrid's relationship to him.

"Thank you. I hope she didn't mind." Perhaps if she kept him talking about the woman, he would eventually say something to bring some light into the matter.

"Not at all. Don't worry about it."

Mm. It seemed she would have to ask a direct question if she wanted a better answer. But she could not work up the courage. After all, it was none of her concern who he and Ingrid were to one another. She should just stop worrying about it.

"I think I'll get changed now."

Though she had intended this as a dismissal, Magnus didn't move. Did he mean to stay here while she removed the shirt and got dressed into the clothes he'd found for her? Agnes shuffled toward the window. Suddenly the sizeable forge seemed too small for two people. Had she been too hasty in thinking he posed no threat to her?

"Forgive me," he said when he saw her retreat. "You have nothing to fear from me. I will go now."

Her heartbeat calmed instantly. She had *not* been too hasty in trusting he would never be any danger to her. "I will be as quick as I can. I know you have to work. And I'm sorry about this morning."

"Sorry?" He blinked.

"I always wake up before dawn, and I didn't think anyone would be up at this hour. I didn't mean to..."

Her voice trailed. She hadn't meant to what? Startle him? But she hadn't. She'd been the one almost jumping out of her skin when she'd seen him in the forge. Embarrass him? It could not be, when she had been the one naked. Scare him? No, he hadn't looked in the least frightened when she'd walked into the room. Rather... transfixed.

"There's no need to apologize. I will now know that you wake up as early as I do, and I will knock before entering the forge."

"Yes. Thank you. Do you think we could we forget what happened?"

He stared at her a long moment. The look on his face seemed to say: "We can try. But I'm not sure we'll succeed."

Which was her opinion also. But it was worth a try. At long last, he answered.

"Of course. It's already forgotten."

With those words, he nodded, and left.

CHAPTER TWO

N ails.

That was what he would make this morning. Nothing too technical, nothing too complex, nothing that would be ruined by his lack of concentration. Magnus stoked up the fire with renewed intent. Today he was only fit to do something he could have done in his sleep, and anyway, people always needed nails, didn't they? It would not be a lost endeavor.

As he worked, he tried his best not to think of Agnes' delightful body, or imagine her washing her clothes. What would have happened if Wolf had asked for the hammer last night instead of this morning? He would have walked in on her naked, bent over the bucket, the most arousing scene he could imagine. His shaft went as hard as the poker in his hand at the thought. He'd seen how perfect her rounded ass was this morning when she'd fled to her room. Such a sight was enough to make a man want to—

A vicious curse escaped Magnus' lips when a hot piece of metal singed his skin, calling him back to the reality of what he was doing. Nails. He'd purposefully chosen to make nails because he'd thought he could do them with his eyes closed.

Apparently, he'd been mistaken.

Staring at the long welt on his arm, he muttered under his breath. How long had it been since he'd injured himself while working? Years. He was usually able to focus and not allow his mind to wander over delectable women or anything else when he handled white-hot metal. He cursed again, louder, and threw the tongs to the floor in an angry gesture. A moment later, the door of the forge opened.

"Is everything all right?" Agnes walked in gingerly, as if unsure of the reception she would get. "I was outside, milking the goat, and I heard—"

"Yes," he cut in. "Everything's fine."

That was a lie.

Everything was most decidedly *not* all right. But he couldn't tell her the truth, couldn't say he'd been obsessing about her naked body, imagining every inch of

delicate spine, from her slender neck to her perfect
buttocks, as she bent over the bucket of water. It was
already a miracle she wasn't afraid of him after what
had happened this morning. It wasn't difficult to guess
he'd looked like a predator in front of his prey when
he'd seen her in her glorious nudity. And then later,
when he'd brought her Ingrid's clothes, he had been
unable to stop himself from staring at her lovely form.
Seeing her clad only in his shirt had been both intimate
and arousing, the perfect combination to make him lose
his mind.

"It's nothing," he said gruffly. "I burned my arm,
that's all."

He was a smithy. He worked with fire. There was
nothing more normal than for a man like him getting
burned, so he hoped the explanation would not raise any
further comment.

But, to his surprise, Agnes looked horrified, as if he
had just admitted to having been bitten by a rabid dog.
"We need to bathe the wound!" she exclaimed, dragging
him by the arm. "Without delay. It's the only way to
prevent the burn from spreading. Come, before it's too
late."

He had no choice but to follow her. For such a slight
woman she was impossible to stop. As he didn't want to
risk hurting her, he did not dare restrain her in any way,

so he let her lead him outside and plunge his hand into a bucket of water she had placed by the fence.

"It's lucky that I've just been to the well to draw some fresh water," she explained, keeping his arm submerged in the cool liquid. "The cold will help with pain as well. Then if you have some honey, we will apply some on the burn once the skin has dried. Where do you find your honey? In the forest yonder, I imagine. Do you know, it's one of my favorite things to eat in the morning."

The sentences ran into each other without pause. It seemed to Magnus that she was trying to prevent an awkward silence from settling between them, which made sense. They were within kissing distance of each other, and their hands were touching under water, a somewhat disturbing sensation. The situation was admittedly more intimate than their short acquaintance warranted.

"I will show you the hive tomorrow, if you want," he rasped, looking at her straight in the eye. "You'll be able to have all the honey you want while you stay with me, not only in the mornings."

The promise sounded more solemn than he'd intended, almost like a pledge.

After a while, the burning sensation eased. He sighed in relief but Agnes made a sound he interpreted as disapproval when she turned his arm over so she could look at the inside of his wrist.

"I'm afraid it will leave a mark."

Yes. He already knew it would. This. Their meeting. The pressure of her fingers on his skin, the way she was taking care of him. No one took care of him, ever, or worried about the injuries he might incur, or the scars it would leave, and he wasn't sure how to handle it.

Magnus tensed. It was subtle, but unmistakable. His hand, so pliable only a moment ago, was now heavy and cumbersome. Agnes gulped, suddenly very aware of their proximity, and of his strength. With that hand he could have choked the life out of her. With that arm, as thick and hard as a piece of wood, he could have sent her sprawling to the floor with one swipe.

"I've never met anyone as wild as you are," she whispered, disentangling her fingers from his. What was she doing, touching a stranger so intimately, bringing her face so close to his?

"Wild?" He sounded affronted by her choice of words. "Like a beast, you mean? Is that what you think of me?"

"No!" She was horrified to have offended him because she had actually meant the word as a compliment. He was wild like a proud wolf roaming the land where he belonged, not bothering to try and join the pack of domesticated dogs. He was wild in the sense that he was not playing any game or pretending to be anything else than what he was at heart. He was strong and free. "The men in my village were all the same, tame and boring and predictable. You, on the other hand, seem..."

She floundered when she realized that, once again, the word that came to her mind was "wild," in the best possible way. But he had not seemed to like it, so she had better not risk repeating it.

"It's all right. You don't have to explain yourself. If that's what you think then there must be a reason." Magnus put an end to her embarrassment by asking a question. "Anyway, why is it that you know so much about burns and how to treat them?"

She reddened. "Because I've been burned on more than one occasion myself."

"How come? You're no blacksmith."

She understood from the way he frowned that he was worried the burns had been inflicted by someone in her family. This proof that he worried about her warmed her. But no, no one had hurt her. Not in that way, at least.

"I was rather clumsy, growing up, so I ended up with my share of scrapes and burns." She lifted the hem of her skirts to show him what she meant. Only when

Magnus' eyes caught fire did she realize what she was doing. Feeling caught out, she covered herself once more. Of course she could not bare her legs to a man thus! What was she thinking? Wasn't it enough that he had seen her naked earlier that day?

But Magnus didn't seem surprised by her willingness to expose herself, or even eager to see her leg. He seemed only concerned to see the extent of her injuries.

"Show me," was all he said.

Slowly, she uncovered her lower leg to show him the white patch in the middle of her calf. It was about the size of her hand, puckered and wrinkled. She had always hated it and could not explain the odd urge to show it to Magnus but the way he looked at it made her think it was nothing to be ashamed of.

"This is the worst one," she whispered, moved by his reaction.

"What happened?"

"I dropped a bucket of boiling water over my leg when I was about eight or nine, while making pottage for the family. It hurt like the devil."

"Yes, it would have." Magnus looked so appalled she could not help a laugh. Hadn't he suffered much worse at the forge? Then the laughter got stuck in her throat when he asked, "Why were you the one hefting buckets of boiling water when you were aged only eight? It seems to me you were not clumsy, you were simply too young for the task."

That was one way of seeing it. And it was true she had not burned herself as much later on in life, when she had been older and strong enough to see to her household chores adequately. But she had not been given the luxury of choice. In her father's mind, a girl had to work to feed the family, and that was that. Her age was irrelevant.

"Not all of them are as bad," she reassured him.

"Show me."

There it was again, the quiet order, as if he had every right to see parts of her body no one else ever saw. It caused her to shiver, because, well, he had seen all of it only this morning. "I can't. They're... not in a place I can easily show you."

Or modestly.

From the way he let his gaze roam over her, she guessed he was trying to imagine where the other scars would be. She had the sudden, mad idea of making him kiss each and every one of them, starting with the one on her shoulder blade before allowing his lips to glide down her back in search of the one on her left hip and then opening her legs so he could lick the small one on the inside of her thigh.

She shivered at the scandalous thought.

"How many scars are we talking about?" His beautiful eyes, usually so blue, had gone the color of a dusky sky. His voice, already rough, had gone the texture of tree bark. She shivered again. Yes, wild did not begin to describe the man.

"It's not as bad as you think. Only three more."

"Three too many, then."

"I wager you have suffered more, being a blacksmith." To illustrate her point, she lifted his arm, turning it this way and that, exposing the white streaks crisscrossing his forearm.

His muscles flexed. My. He was so strong, and, yes, so wild. It always came back to this with him. She had never seen men like him. Even Björn, who had struck her at first, when she'd met him in her village, didn't have this rough edge. Was it because he was older? Because he worked with fire and made sparks fly with his hammer, like a demonic, untameable creature? She didn't know. But he drew her like nothing else.

"Yes. I have suffered more burns than you," he said, removing his arm from her grasp. "But it's not the same. I asked for it."

"No one asks to be hurt, or deserves to be."

He plunged his gaze into hers. For a moment it looked as if he would say something. Then he thought better of it and stood back up.

"Come. Let's find that honey."

THE NEXT TWO days were spent in easy companionship.

To Magnus' delight, Agnes turned out to be an efficient helper. Not in the forge per se, as he refused to have someone who'd already suffered her share of burns anywhere near the scorching fire or the bellows. But she allowed him to focus on his work by talking to the people coming by, handling payments and making notes of what the villagers commissioned. Her way of doing it was ingenious and endearing at the same time. One evening he'd found a chain on his workbench, arranged in an unusual shape.

"What is that?" he asked, arching a brow.

"Oh. A man called Arne came to ask if you could make him a chain to hang a cooking pot over the fire. You were busy hammering away so I put one here because I did not want to forget to tell you."

"You did not just put it there, though, did you. You arranged it there." There was no mistaking her effort at disposing it in an artistic manner.

"Yes. In the shape of a bird. He told me his name meant 'eagle'."

"Oh, so that's a *bird*? I was wondering."

The teasing had the desired effect. Agnes blushed a delicious color. "Yes, or at least, it was supposed to be. I thought it would help me remember who requested the chain, as it seemed important to deliver the message accurately. I wanted to be useful."

Something in his heart fluttered. "I'm sorry. I shouldn't have mocked you. This was very kind and clever of you. Let's hope next time you don't speak to Wolf."

To his relief, she smiled. "Yes. A wolf's head would be rather hard to recreate."

The next day he'd found five nails in a woven basket. The thing that had fluttered in his chest the day before stretched its wings again.

"Let me guess. Sigurd came?" The man had a talent for basket weaving, so it made sense. "How many nails does he want?"

"Fifty. I thought the long nails would represent ten, the short ones one."

"Very good. If you carry on like this, I won't want you to leave," he told her as they sat down to eat. "You are far too valuable to me. You help while I work and you ensure I eat like a king as well. That mushroom stew is excellent."

He chewed on his mouthful thoughtfully. It was true that she was a helpful companion, and a talented cook, but that was not the reason why he wanted her to stay. It was good having her with him and he felt sure he would have felt the same had she been useless in the forge or in the kitchen.

"It's nothing," she said in her usual shy manner. "And you roasted the partridge to perfection. How did you even catch it? I didn't see you take any sling or bow or anything this morning."

"I don't need anything. I just use stones."

"Stones?"

He shrugged. "From a young age I have hunted birds with stones. It amused me to test my accuracy, and I have become quite adept at it."

"Will you show me how you do that?"

"Why? You don't believe me?" He let out a short laugh he regretted when she flushed to the roots of her hair.

"N-no, it's only... I've never heard of anyone doing that before and I—"

"I know. Forgive me. More stew?" he asked, hoping to regain the ease between them. Why was he constantly teasing her and making her ill at ease? One of these days he might go too far.

Agnes shook her head and nodded toward his left wrist instead. "How is the burn?"

"Much better, thank you."

It was better. He only noticed it because every time he did, it made him think of how she had taken care of him. More than once he'd thought that he would gladly singe his whole body if it meant her running her fingers over him to soothe the burn.

"Show me."

The same two words he'd told her the other day. Why did they sound so arousing? He had no idea.

When he made no move to obey, she came to stand by his stool. His breath hitched in his chest because in that position, his mouth was level with her maddening breasts, the perfect shape of which he had not been able to forget. Did she have no fear, coming to him like this? Wasn't she worried about what he might do? Not that he would ever hurt her, of course, but there were still many a thing he could do to her, things he *wanted* to do to her. Slowly, his gaze never leaving hers, he lifted the cuff of his shirt. His whole body tensed when she took his wrist to turn it around and expose the burn.

"It's not too bad," she murmured. "I think the honey helped."

"Yes."

He had to go, now, or he would do something unwise. Draw her onto his lap to run his hands all over her too tempting body, grab the back of her neck to kiss her too luscious mouth, rip the bodice of her dress open to suckle her too perfect breasts. The possibilities were endless, each worse than the other.

He stood up, feeling ten feet tall in front of her, and wild, just as she'd said the other day. And though he'd not been sure what to make of the word at the time, he now understood it had been a compliment. Because the difference in stature and appearance between them was undeniably arousing. It highlighted both his masculinity and her femininity, intensified the tension between them and made their proximity all the more explosive.

Together they would set the sheets on fire, he was certain of it.

He took a step back, warding off the temptation to put the shocking thought to the test there and then.

"Well, good night then, Agnes."

She bit her bottom lip and he almost broke through his self-imposed restraint. Would it be so bad to reach for her? To draw her into his arms and—

"Good night, Magnus."

CHAPTER THREE

The bucket was heavier than she had anticipated, she should not have crammed it so full. Agnes gritted her teeth. Another few steps and she would be inside the forge. Surely she would be able to make it to the table? It was not so far.

Just as she passed the door, she stumbled and ended up crashing against the door frame leading to her room. The bucket fell at her feet, scattering turnips and onions everywhere, Panting, she thanked her lucky stars the door had been opened. She would have smashed head-first against the wood panel otherwise.

When she finally felt steady enough to move, she found that she could not. Damnation, the back of her dress had caught on something she could not even see and she could not reach it to disentangle herself.

As she debated what to do, the door to the forge opened behind her. Thank God, Magnus was here. She had started to fear she would have to rip Ingrid's dress to free herself. Her new friend had assured her she was in no hurry to get the dress back but Agnes had no intention of giving it back with a big rip in it.

"Could you come in here a moment?" she called out, guessing he would not have realized the situation she was in. "I'm trapped."

It was ridiculous to ask for help for such a thing, but she hadn't managed to free herself, no matter how much she'd tried, so she might as well ask for Magnus' help. Better to sacrifice her pride than tear a garment that did not belong to her.

A hand landed on the small of her back, warm and strong. "Trapped, are we?"

Agnes stilled. Was this really Magnus? Suddenly she wasn't so sure. He felt just as massive behind her, and he'd entered the forge as if he had every right to, but his touch felt odd, and his voice sounded somehow lighter than the blacksmith's, with a mocking edge she had never heard before and that made her uncomfortable. He might tease her, but he never made her feel inadequate.

She twisted around and gasped. It wasn't Magnus at all, even if he looked very similar. But since her arrival in the village she'd had chance to see that all the men here were tall, blond and muscular. No wonder in the corner of her eye she hadn't seen anything suspicious.

"My dress got caught on a nail or a hook or something as I brushed past the door," she explained, wishing now she had not called out to him. The hand poised on her lower back seemed to have burned a hole through the wool of her gown.

"Mmm, yes, so I see. What will you give me as a reward for freeing you?"

"Reward?"

"Yes," he purred, oblivious to the strangled sound she gave. "I think you should make it worth my while, don't you?"

"No." The word darted out of her mouth. After all, she was not asking for anything too taxing.

Instead of backing away, he laughed at her answer. "A spirited one, hey. My brother will have his hands full with you."

"You're Magnus' brother?" Now she understood the similarities between them. He was not just any Norseman, he was the brother she had heard mentioned a few times.

"Sven. At your service."

"Then if you are, please, would you unhook my dress? I don't want to damage it any further."

"I can certainly help you... remove it altogether."

The hand at her back slid lower. Everything within Agnes tightened. She was trapped, literally. If he wanted to tear the dress from her or claim his "reward", as he'd called it, for helping her out, she could do nothing. Even if she had been free of her movements, the man was too massive for her to have a chance at escaping his lust.

Her heart started to beat a frantic rhythm. What was she to do?

"Sven?"

The voice cut through the panic building inside her. She had been about to snatch at the dress, and run away, regardless of the state of it. She was sure Ingrid would have understood, when she explained her predicament.

"Magnus. Here you are, bursting in at the worst possible moment, as ever." The glee in Sven's voice as he told his brother he was not welcome grated on Agnes' already frayed nerves. There was animosity there, not just good-natured teasing. "Do you think you could give us a moment? I was about to see to the girl's dress."

No, no, *no*! He'd made it sound as if the undressing would happen with her full agreement and they would tumble into bed afterward. She tried to turn around to face Magnus, explain what was really going on, but with her dress caught she could not move as she wanted and, try as she might, she could not see past the man standing right behind her.

The man who still had his hand over the swell of her buttocks.

"It's not what you think, my dress snagged on a nail when I walked too close to the door frame just now," she blurted out. "And I could not seem to unhook it on my own, so I—"

"Yes," Sven snapped, as if he hadn't enjoyed her cutting through his explanation. "As I said, I was about to help her remove—"

"*I* will do that, and *you* will wait outside."

The words were little more than a growl and all of a sudden the man blocking her view vanished, presumably pushed away by a hulking blacksmith. A heartbeat later Magnus was standing in his place, just as tall, just as forbidding, but not half as frightening. All the tension left Agnes' body in one rush. With him she was safe. He would help, and he would not rip her dress to shreds or throw her on the bed to claim any dubious reward afterward.

As if to prove her right, Magnus started to tug at the material of her gown without a word. Anger was radiating from his body, an anger she wasn't sure was directed at Sven. It might be directed at her. A moment later, she was free.

Not daring to face his ire, she kept her back to him. "I swear nothing was about to—"

"You and Sven can do what you want."

"But I do not *want* to do anything with him! That's the problem," she cried out, turning around at last. She could not bear to have him think she had been about to beg his brother to take her to bed. "He made it sound as if I did, but I don't. I would have run away, only, I was trapped, as you saw, and he—"

"Did he touch you?"

"N-no." But he might well have, had Magnus not arrived. She would not have put it past the man and his hand had already been on her, in much too low a place to pass as innocent. However she did not think it a good idea to point it out to Magnus, who already sounded mightily aggrieved. "He only scared me. For a moment I didn't know what to think. I'm not even sure he wanted to do anything other than tease me or upset you."

"I'm sorry he scared you. Sven is..."

Magnus let out a sigh instead of finishing the sentence but she thought she understood all the same. Sven enjoyed getting the upper hand over his brother, and he'd jumped on the opportunity to upset him. She had only been a tool in his petty games, most likely he'd felt no real desire for her.

"You're right, he wouldn't have hurt you, he's not a

dangerous man. But for all that, he enjoys riling me, and if he thought that you and I... That is, if he thought you were my..." He waved his hand as if unable to find an acceptable way to say what he wanted to say. Again, there was no need. She understood all too well. Sven had thought the two of them were lovers. "There has always been this competition between us, and he is confident in the fact that he nearly always wins. He will have wanted to see if he could make you choose him instead of me."

"Yes, I think that's exactly what he wanted," Agnes said in a breath. *My brother will have his hands full with you.* That was what he'd said, which proved he'd thought they were a couple. She shuddered at the man's presumption and forgot to be embarrassed. He'd thought she was his brother's lover, and yet he had tried to seduce her. Magnus was right. He did like to rile him and get the upper hand over him. How despicable. "But how could he suppose I would do such a thing? Prefer him to you?"

If she really had been involved with Magnus, why on earth would she have jeopardized what they had for a man she didn't even know, who was arrogance personified?

There was a silence before Magnus answered. "Because most people do."

"Most people?"

"Our parents, for one. Sven has always been the perfect, oldest son. Perhaps because he is the image of my father, in looks and personality, he's always been the favorite. I was only ever a replacement at best, a disappointment at worst." He made a grimace. "It's not just them, though. I told you. People usually do not choose me."

Agnes stared at him in disbelief. Who in their right mind would choose anyone over him? Much less an overbearing, overconfident braggard? In her opinion, there was no contest.

She shivered, and Magnus took a step forward. They were now almost touching but she didn't step back. She would never step back from this man.

"Are you sure you're all right? He didn't frighten you too badly? I saw how he was holding you." He growled, as if the idea displeased him.

"A-a little." There was no point in lying. When she had felt the man's hand on her and heard him talk about rewards, she had taken fright. For a moment it had looked as if her worst nightmare had come true. "But then you arrived. I'm all right."

She stayed very still, resisting the urge to burrow into his chest. It was not just the relief of having him come to her aid that made her want to hug him, it was the pain she'd heard in his voice when he'd said no one ever chose him. She knew about that, about never being seen as worth considering. Magnus appeared so different from her, so much stronger, she'd had no idea that they would have this in common.

He nodded, as if thinking the same thing and not knowing what to do with the revelation either. Then he seemed to get hold of himself and looked at the chaos in the room.

"Why are there are turnips and onions everywhere?" His lips quivered. "Did a Saxon farmer come to request a metal fence to put around his vegetable patch in my absence?"

She smiled at the jest, enjoying the restored companionship between them. "No. It's all my fault, I stumbled and dropped the bucket I was carrying. I'm sorry. I told you I was clumsy."

"No." His smile vanished as he took in the quantity of vegetables on the floor. "You simply take on tasks you should leave to other people. Next time you have to carry such a heavy bucket, you call me, you understand?"

"I will."

An awkward silence settled between them. It felt as if they had made a much more significant pledge.

"Now. The room where you sleep is the one I usually give Sven when he visits. Of course he could always come sleep in the hut with me this time." Magnus started to rub at the back of his neck, the gesture betraying intense discomfort. She had seen enough of the two brothers to understand why he never welcomed him under his roof and would prefer to keep it that way.

"It's not a problem. Let him sleep where he usually sleeps. I can sleep with you. I mean..." Heat flooded her cheeks when she realized how it sounded. "I mean in your hut."

"You would do that?"

"Of course. It's better than a ditch in the forest."

Magnus recoiled as violently as if she had slapped him. "If one of us had to sleep in a ditch, it would be me, not you!"

She could not help a smile at his vehemence. How had he not seen it was a jest? "But neither of us has to sleep outside, that's my point. I trust you."

The declaration had moved him, she could tell from the way his eyes glimmered. Her own chest tightened in turn. But, of course, she trusted him. She felt as if she had known him all her life.

"I'll go prepare a pallet for you in my hut, then. Thank you."

Magnus was still trembling when he exited the forge, overset by a mixture of anticipation at the idea of having Agnes under his roof, gratitude at the trust she had gifted him with and anger at his brother's behavior toward her. The way he'd held her had been highly inappropriate. No wonder she'd taken fright. As to his own reaction, blind rage, it was perhaps less easily explicable.

Outside, Sven was waiting, a smirk on his face, looking not guilty in the least.

"Well, now, little br—"

"What are you doing here?" Magnus cut in. He was not in the mood to endure any teasing from him today, and certainly not about Agnes. When he had seen his brother bent over her, as if about to kiss her neck, and heard him talk about removing her dress, his blood had run cold.

No, not her, his whole body had protested. Sven could seduce all the women he wanted, but he could not touch her, he could tease him as he usually did, but he had better not cause her a moment's discomfort. His ire and determination must have shown on his face, because Sven answered his question seriously, as if knowing that doing anything else would earn him a fist in the face.

"I came to ask for Wolf's advice."

Of course. How had Magnus not guessed? The Icelander was the first port of call for the Norsemen around. Once he'd become a man, Sven had elected to go and live in a Saxon village alone, but every now and then he still needed to consult with Wolf on some issue or another.

"How long will you stay?"

"Not long. I will leave tomorrow." Sven tilted his head. "Tell you what, you can take me back home in your cart. 'Tis a rather long walk from the village to here."

Magnus scoffed. How like Sven to assume he would just do his bidding. "I have work here, you know. I can't just leave on a whim."

"It would not be the first time you've done it."

"No, but—"

Just then the door opened on Agnes. He saw from the way she blushed she had not expected to find them so close to the forge and would have stayed inside if she'd known where they were. He gave her a reassuring smile and turned to face Sven again.

"I'm not taking you all the way back home," he said, switching from Norse for her benefit. The last thing he wanted was for her to be ill at ease when she imagined them talking or even arguing about her. "I have done on occasion when I happened to have business in town, but I don't this time."

"People always need something or other from town," Sven said with an exasperated wave of the hand. "Why can't you be like anyone else for once?"

There was small inhale of breath from his left side. Agnes. He might not have heard it coming from someone else but somehow his senses seemed to be attuned to her. He turned to address her once more.

"Do you have need of going into town?" It was the only thing he could think of to explain the way her eyes had suddenly brightened, as if in expectation.

"I-I could do with buying a few items," she admitted in a whisper. "I left home rather precipitously."

Of course. How had he not thought of that? Why, she was this very moment wearing a dress belonging to another woman. She would welcome the opportunity to get some things for herself.

"Very well," he agreed. "We'll leave early in the morning."

Sven let out a burst of laughter. "You will do for her what you will not do for me, I see," he said, reversing back to Norse. "Well, I cannot say I blame you. She's quite a pretty—"

"Shut your mouth," Magnus snarled in the same language. "And if I see you put your hand, or even just a finger on her ever again, I will cut it and feed it to my dog. Is that understood?"

The outburst was so unprecedented that Sven did not even think to smirk. Satisfaction swelled within

Magnus. Why had he not done that before? It was not so difficult to put his brother back in his place.

"Understood. Now, shall we go and see Wolf? What I have to tell him will be of interest to you."

"You go. I'll join you in a moment."

First, he had to prepare a pallet for Agnes in his hut. At the idea of her sleeping so near him, his body gave a jolt. *Another* jolt, he should say. He seemed to be constantly aroused around her.

That decided him.

Instead of joining her as quickly as possible, as he would have liked to do, he would stay drinking and talking with Wolf and Sven long into the night. He would wait until she was safely asleep before going back home. That way he would not risk doing something stupid, like pouncing on her as soon as she looked at him in that way she had of looking at him.

Yes.

That was what he would do. Talk to distract his mind from thoughts of Agnes, drink to dull the edge of the desire he felt for her, and hope it worked.

CHAPTER FOUR

The moon was high in the sky when Magnus finally made his way back to his hut. His plan had worked. It was the middle of the night. By now Agnes should be asleep, safe in the corner he had prepared for her, as far away from his pallet as it was possible to be while staying within the confines of the hut.

Careful not to wake her, he opened the door inch by inch. Nothing. He let out a silent sigh of relief. She was sleeping, as he'd hoped, and not standing stark naked in the middle of the room. It was safe to come in. Avoiding looking in the corner in case a beam of moonlight revealed a part of her all too tempting body, he collapsed onto his bed—and almost flattened the woman lying on it.

"Agnes!" He instantly rolled off her, shock radiating from his every pore. "What are you doing here?"

"Magnus?" She sounded bewildered, as if he'd just woken her, nervous, as if she feared his intent, and slightly breathless, as if he'd crushed her under this bulk. A dreadful combination. "You t-told me to sleep in your hut tonight, don't you remember?"

"Of course I remember. But I didn't mean you should sleep in my bed!" He sounded gruffer than he wanted but his control was hanging by a thread. Feeling her warm, soft body under him had been a shock he'd not been prepared for.

"I'm sorry, I thought that one was your bed?" She gestured at the pallet in the corner.

"No. That's the one I prepared for you." He had piled it high with blankets and furs to make it as comfortable and inviting as possible. How had she not guessed this would be the one allocated to her? He was a man, he didn't need all that comfort around him.

"Forgive me. I'll go to it then, and leave you to sleep in your own bed."

His hand shot out of its own accord. When his fingers made contact with her wrist they wrapped around it like a shackle. Her impossibly delicate, fragile wrist. He forced himself to ease the grip. "No, Agnes. Stay. Please."

There was a pause while she absorbed what he'd said. All he could see in the darkness was her shadowy form, all he could hear was his heart drumming in his chest. What would she do now? Would she scream and flee in fright at the demand? To his relief, she did neither.

Instead she asked. "Why do you want me to stay?"

He had no answer to that question. He had no idea where the request had come from, because he was not drunk, and he certainly had no intention of taking advantage of the fact that they would sleep next to one another. "I don't know. It just feels right to have you here with me. You have nothing to fear, I swear I won't take advantage of you."

She stared at him, her eyes glittering in the moonlight. Had he ever seen a more beautiful woman, he wondered for the hundredth time? He might have, but not a more compelling one.

"I believe you," she said eventually.

"So you will stay?"

"Yes."

A joy the likes of which he'd never felt before, quiet and all the more perfect for it, spread through his chest. "Let me go get more blankets and furs from the other pallet, so you can be comfortable."

"I already am."

Ignoring her protests, he stood up and went to the other side of the room. He would not have her inconvenienced in any way. When he came back, he made a nest for her, next to his sleeping place. She lay on it without hesitation and closed her eyes. Feeling more content than he had ever felt, he settled himself next to her.

"Did I hurt you when I fell on you?"

"No."

"I'm three times as heavy as you are, I must have—"

"You didn't." She sounded half asleep already. "I'm all right. So warm and comfortable here."

"Let us sleep then."

He gave a rueful smile. As if he would be able to sleep with her by his side, so close to his heaving chest. But to his surprise, he was soon overcome by an irresistible torpor and he did fall into a deep, dreamless sleep.

In the morning, Agnes woke with her hand in Magnus'. She could not recall reaching out to him in her sleep or him asking if he could hold her. But here they were, fingers entwined, and it felt good.

Natural.

He was still asleep, his head thrown to the side, his

other hand resting over his chest. The sight was oddly moving. Feeling privileged to be allowed to do so while he was oblivious, she examined him, taking her time. His beard, in particular, fascinated her. Saxon men tended to be clean-shaven, and right now she couldn't think why they would choose not to grow beards. But, of course, it might not suit them as well as it suited Magnus. Because suit him it did. The golden hairs provided the perfect frame for his sensual mouth. They looked so soft she almost reached out to stroke them. And his full lips were so tempting, she fought the urge to place her own over them.

Instinct told her it would be both the most satisfying experience of her life and the most dangerous, because kissing a virile man like him could only lead to more. But right now, he was asleep, so perhaps she could dare? She leaned over, irresistibly drawn. Could she—

The furious banging on the door tore a shriek from her lips.

Jolted awake, Magnus bolted into a sitting position, and as she was so close to him, his head almost collided with hers.

"What the—" A sentence in Norse, coming from the other side of the door cut him off and he barked a brief answer in the same language. "It's Sven," he explained, glancing at the window through which the sun was pouring into the hut. "It's much later than I thought it was," he mumbled, sounding caught out.

Agnes' consternation matched his own. Lost to her contemplation of his perfect face, she had not realized what time it was. But they had said they would leave early, so it was no wonder his brother was wondering where they were.

"We should go," she said guiltily. If she had not agreed to sleep next to him, she was certain neither of them would have overslept.

She made to get up but Magnus caught her by the wrist, much in the same way he had done the night before. The heat of his fingers over her chilled skin was delicious. The night had been unseasonably cold and she found herself wishing he could warm her all over.

"No, wait... Just another moment, please."

What was this? He wanted her in his bed, but not as a lover. He wanted to lie next to her, not over her. He had made no move to seduce her last night, as promised. So what did this mean? What did he want?

She lay back down on the pallet, waiting, guessing there was something on his mind.

"I like having you in my hut," he said eventually. It sounded like a confession. "I've never lived with anyone and it's nice."

It was. The only people she had lived with, her own

family, had seen her as little more than a servant, they had mocked, used, or just plain ignored her. With Magnus, it was different. She could be herself, and her efforts were appreciated. He liked what she cooked, he was grateful for her help at the forge, small though it may be, and he never demanded she do anything. Quite the opposite. He was going out of his way to see to her comfort. Like he had last night with the pallet.

Unable to resist, she snuggled up closer to him. "I'm cold," she said by way of an explanation. It was not exactly a lie, even if she was in no danger of freezing.

"Come here."

A huge arm wrapped around her shoulders. The gesture was as natural as if they'd slept together a thousand times and she pressed herself against his chest, relishing the sense of security it gave her.

"You're so warm," she mumbled, wondering if she was not about to fall back to sleep. There was a rumble against her cheek. It took her a moment to understand that Magnus was laughing.

"I suppose I spend so much time by the fire that the heat has seeped into me."

"Mm. Maybe." Whatever the explanation for it, she already knew she would want to snuggle up next to him every night, which was problematic. There was no guarantee he would want to have her in his bed tomorrow night or indeed any other night.

With reluctance, Magnus let go of Agnes. She fit so perfectly against his flank that he could have stayed entwined with her all day long but it was high time they left, if they wanted to go into town and be back to the village before nightfall.

Bloody Sven.

"I suppose I had better go get the cart ready."

He barely resisted the urge to place a kiss on her forehead before he got up. The impulse was odd to say the least. Since when did he kiss women on the forehead? He had only ever kissed them on the lips or in the sweet place between their legs, in the heat of passion. This would have been different, a proof of tenderness and respect, and he didn't quite know what to make of it.

He took a swig of ale before exiting the hut. Sven was waiting outside, idly cleaning his nails with a twig. His mouth curled up when he spotted him.

"Sleep well, little brother?" Never had Magnus wanted to wipe the smirk off anyone's face more. "What happened to the industrious blacksmith who wakes up at dawn? Did he find something better to do? I wonder what that might be. Or maybe I don't." The wretched man waggled his brows.

"I told you yesterday to shut your mouth," he

growled. "I suggest you keep it shut or you might find yourself with a dislocated jaw before long."

Sven seemed about to reply, then thought the better of it. Perhaps he had seen that this was no idle threat. "Where did you find her anyway? You've had your share of women, but I've never seen you with a Saxon before."

"There's a first time for everything."

Why had he answered as if he and Agnes were really a couple, Magnus wondered? Oh well. Too late to rectify the impression now, Sven was already convinced they were involved, and if it helped keep his filthy hands from her, then all the better. Not that he had much hope his brother would heed his warning. He never did.

"A bit young for you, is she not?"

"She's no child," Magnus said defensively before thinking the better of his reaction. Sven was only trying to rile him again. He should be ignoring the taunts. "She's slight, it is not the same."

He knew Agnes to be about Björn's age, which was admittedly younger than his usual conquests, but old enough to be bedding him. Not that they were sleeping together, of course...

The thought did little to appease his anger, because he wished they were, and not just to hold hands.

"Mm. If you say so." Sven threw the twig away with a flick of the wrist.

"I do. Now, I thought you were eager to leave." He strode in the direction of the stable where his mare was waiting. "So let's go."

SETTLED between two enormous Norsemen Agnes was intimidated into silence. She let them talk above her head about people she didn't know and places she had never visited. For once, she wished they were talking in Norse, as it would have given her the perfect excuse not to join in the conversation, but Magnus insisted they talked in her language when in her presence. The intention found favor with her but there was no denying she was ill at ease and fast regretting her request to go into town. Why had she told Magnus she could do with buying a few items there? It was true, but she should perhaps have waited for a more opportune moment to go. The latent animosity between the two men was making her uncomfortable. She felt like a rabbit caught between two snarling beasts.

"What brought you to a village of Norsemen then, Agnes?" Sven asked her after a while. Had he been anyone else she might have thought he was trying to make her feel less excluded. But she guessed he was merely looking for another way to rile his brother.

Evidently, he thought she had come here to be with Magnus and wondered how a man like him could possibly have attracted her.

She decided to put the insufferable man back in his place. If she *had* decided to come here to be with Magnus, then it would be the best decision she had ever made, and she would be sure to leave him in no doubt about it.

After all he had made his brother endure, he had it coming.

"Björn and Dunne came to visit my village a few weeks ago and offered me the opportunity to travel south with them. I accepted, not knowing what was waiting for me, but considering what I found, I'm mighty glad I did. I'm not sure I will ever go home now."

For good measure, she threw an adoring glance at Magnus, one that caused heat to flush to her cheeks. In normal circumstances, she might have been embarrassed, but right now she didn't mind, as it only added to the effect she was trying to create. The smile she got in return was blinding. Magnus had seen what she was doing and was grateful for her efforts. But she was glad to help when it cost her little. Besides, nothing she'd said had been a lie. She was glad to have accepted Björn's offer and she truly had no intention of going back home.

John the miller's father would be waiting for her there, or another of her father's vile friends.

It didn't bear thinking about.

She spent the rest of the journey with a strong thigh pressed close against hers.

Finally, they reached the town. It was bustling with activity. Agnes looked around, aghast. She had never been in such a big, busy place and found it hard to adjust to the noisy crowd and so many comings and goings.

"It's market day." Magnus had not missed her reaction. "Forgive me, I didn't think to tell you. Is it a problem?" he asked in a lower voice, leaning toward her while Sven jumped off the cart with a satisfied grunt.

"I..." It was not a problem, exactly, but suddenly she wished she was back at the forge with him. This was overwhelming, much more so than she had expected, and she felt rather silly. "I didn't think the town would be so big, that's all."

Magnus nodded, as if understanding what she was not saying. "If you can wait to buy what you need, I'll take you back another day, when it's quieter. Or we can go to the other town on the other side of the forest if you prefer. It's a bit further but not as big. We don't have to stay here if it makes you nervous."

In truth, it did. Having never left her village before Björn's arrival, she was not used to being in such strange surroundings. Everything here was bigger, noisier, more daunting. But how could she tell Magnus that when he had only agreed to come for her sake? He had sacrificed a day's work for her, surrendered to his brother's will for her. She could not make him appear a fool now.

In the end, she didn't have to say anything. He gathered up the reins and called out to Sven, who had started talking to a man selling tanned leather skins.

"You'll make your way home from here," he said, turning the cart around. "'Tis not so far and I would like to get back home before the night sets in. Today being a miserable day there won't be light for much longer, and we set off later than we'd intended."

"Well, whose fault was that?" Sven didn't sound impressed at his brother's defection. "I thought we'd agreed you would take me to—"

"You thought wrong. Goodbye."

Agnes saw from the way Magnus' shoulders relaxed that he was pleased to be the one to dismiss his brother for once and she couldn't help but share in the satisfaction.

"If you'd rather we took him home before getting back to the village, it's no problem," she forced herself to say, though in truth she was relieved to be rid of Sven's oppressive presence. She couldn't wait to be alone with Magnus again.

"No." He gave her a smile that went straight to her heart. "Thank you. This is the first time my brother and I part with me having the upper hand. It feels good, and I owe it to you."

"Me?"

"You gave me a reason to stand up to him. When it was only me, I saw no harm in letting him indulge in his petty games. It seemed to be the way of things, as immutable as the changing of the seasons." He shrugged, before something hardened in his eyes. "But I will not have him making you uncomfortable in any way. And so thanks to you, at last I found the strength to stand up to him. I can only hope it will be the start of a new relationship between us, a more peaceful one. It's about time."

By now a lump had formed in Agnes throat. He was thinking of her, first and foremost, he was being mindful of her comfort again. No one had ever done that before. He was grateful to her for giving him strength when the notion of a woman like her giving a man like him strength should have been ridiculous. She felt on the verge of tears. Magnus saw it and mercifully behaved as if there was nothing more normal in the world than for a woman to cry for no reason.

"Shall we?" he asked, clicking his tongue to the mare.

Agnes could only nod.

CHAPTER FIVE

No sooner had they passed the town gates than the heavens opened.

Agnes let out a cry of dismay when hundreds of cold raindrops hit her all at once. Immediately, Magnus threw one of the furs he had taken with them over her head. She thanked him with a smile, already knowing it would be soaked before they reached the forest. But at least she could not feel the icy pinpricks on her exposed skin anymore, which was a welcome improvement. Would there be no end to his solicitude?

For a moment, they plodded on, in the hope that it would only a be a passing shower but the driving rain showed no sign of abating. On the contrary, it soon became a veritable deluge. Agnes was soon shivering, because as she had predicted, the fur covering her head was now dripping onto her skirt.

"Let us take shelter in that cave over there," Magnus shouted, his voice barely audible above the din.

She nodded her agreement. Even if it was too late to avoid a thorough drenching, at least they would be able to wait out the end of the storm in a dry place.

He helped her down the seat then gestured that she should go into the wide opening while he saw to the horse and cart. She didn't need to be told twice. The cold had started to spread to her bones.

As soon as she entered the cave, she let out a sigh of relief. Oh, this was better. Shaking the fur off her shoulders, she placed it on a rock, then wrung her hair and her sodden skirt. Feeling marginally better, she waited. A moment later, Magnus joined her in the cave.

Agnes' mouth fell open.

Water was falling in rivulets down the strong column of his throat and his clothes were plastered to his body, forcing the eye to follow the lines of each bulging muscle. His wet hair, no longer the color of the sun but now a fascinating metallic hue, seemed longer than usual. Raindrops clung to his lashes, framing his blues eyes with pearls she wanted to lick away. Her tongue was aching with the need to taste his rain-soaked skin, which she suspected would be cold and delicious.

Desperate to resist the shocking impulse, she made the mistake of looking at the ceiling—and that was when she saw them. Bats. Dozens of them, huddled in a nook overhead. A squeal escaped her throat. She'd always been terrified of the animals.

It had started innocently enough. One evening while gathering wood for the fire she'd stayed out later than usual and had ended up surrounded by a cloud of the flying creatures. It had impressed her but she had bravely stopped herself from panicking. Back home she had made the mistake of mentioning the incident to her brothers, who had thought it funny to scare their seven-year-old impressionable sister. The following night she had found their little hut filled with fluttering bats. The boys had locked her in and only allowed her out when their mother had come back home a long moment later and scolded her sons for bringing in animals who had left their droppings and awful smell all over the house.

By then the damage had been done, and Agnes was thoroughly terrified of bats, even if she had gotten out of the hut unscathed.

"What is it?" Magnus started to look around in search of potential danger. He obviously thought she'd identified some potential threat while he was outside.

"Bats," Agnes said, too scared to even think of lying or feel ridiculous.

He lifted his head to the roof of the cave and nodded. "What about them?"

"They're everywhere!" Could he not see?

"Yes. But they're sleeping. It's the middle of the day." He sounded nonplussed. "You don't have anything to fear."

Didn't have anything to fear? On the contrary. She could already hear them flapping around her, feel them scratching at her skin. It was irrational, but she could not help it. Oh, this was awful. She was about to collapse under the strain of trying to hold on to her composure.

Without thinking, Agnes threw herself against Magnus' massive body, hiding her face in his chest. Instantly, he closed his arms around her, keeping her tight against him. Thank God he didn't protest, mock her or even ask any questions. He simply held her, as if he'd sensed she was on the verge of panic and wanted to help. He was so big he completely engulfed her, offering the protection and comfort she needed.

Intent on burrowing further into the embrace, she wiggled against him. Dear God, he felt so warm, so solid, so good. It was exactly what she needed. Thanks to him she was able to distract herself from the horror of being trapped in a cave with bats flying overhead.

Well, she wasn't trapped, exactly, and the animals were still sleeping, but that was by the by.

Slowly, panic receded, and she started to accept she had nothing to fear. The bats were not going anywhere. She was safe.

Magnus was enduring agony. Agnes' warm body pressed against his was putting all sorts of ideas into his head, none of which he should have entertained.

"Agnes, you need to let go of me," he breathed. "If you don't, I might..."

He might what? Tumble her to the floor and thrust into her? Start rubbing himself against her soft stomach to bring about the release he needed? Ask her to kneel at his feet to suck blessed relief out of him? None of these options were advisable but he had fought his desire for her for days, woken up next to her this morning and his control had been worn dangerously thin. He wasn't sure he would be able to resist this last provocation.

She didn't move, didn't draw away. Instead she asked a question. "You might what?"

"Don't ask me that," he said through gritted teeth. Was the woman mad? Couldn't she see she was playing with fire?

This time she did draw back, enough to look at him with eyes the color of a spring leaf. "Because you want me?"

How could he tell her the truth, that he wanted her more than his next breath, had done since the moment he'd seen her naked in his forge? But how could he deny it? He was so hard, it was impossible she hadn't noticed it, pressed as she had been against him. Perhaps admitting to it out loud would help him see how ludicrous this was.

"I do. And it hurts."

"Could I help?"

"Help?" The word was little more than a croak. And then the croak transformed into a gasp when she pressed herself against his aching groin. Was she trying to kill him? Apparently so.

"Yes. I don't want to go back out into the rain but being in here with the bats, even if they aren't moving at present, makes me nervous. Helping you would distract me from my fear."

Distract her. As if that were a viable argument.

"Agnes, women don't pleasure men to distract themselves," he forced himself to answer. Why was he even arguing? Who cared why she wanted to do that as long as she did? Well, *he* cared. He didn't want her to feel constrained in any way, forced to do something she would only regret afterward, if not during. But his body was urging him to do something his mind was telling him was a bad idea and he had no idea which of them would win.

"You said you were in pain, through my fault,

because I threw myself in your arms," she said, sounding both dismayed and aroused at the notion. "It's only fair I help relieve the pain, don't you think?"

A gentle hand landed over his shaft. His aching, pulsing, impossibly hard shaft. And started stroking. All his best intentions flew out of the window. He'd tried to be reasonable, and he'd lost. His fate was now in her hands, quite literally.

He threw his head back and allowed her to ease the pressure pulsing in his veins. Her dainty fingers were offering some relief, but not enough, nowhere near enough.

"For the love of all you Saxons consider holy," he breathed, "if you really are going to do that, please take me in hand. I need to feel your skin on mine."

In truth, he wanted to feel her mouth on him, not her fingers, but there was a limit to what he was prepared to demand from her. It was already a miracle she had not fled out the cave screaming.

"Like this?"

With a dexterity that promised untold delights, and a boldness he would not have credited her with, Agnes unlaced his wet braies. As soon as they'd pooled at his feet, she wrapped her fingers around him. They were warm, and smooth, so smooth. He lost the ability to think and let her explore.

"Show me," she whispered. "I don't know what to do to please a man. I've never done anything like this before."

Forgetting all shame, he placed his own fingers over hers and showed her what to do.

"Yes, this way. Harder. I need..." He was panting now. "Please, Agnes, I need it harder."

He needed to come, now, that was what he needed. Mercifully, she did not ask any questions, take exception to the gruff tone or the crude gestures. She let him guide her and choose the rhythm of the caress. It was so wicked, so much better than when he stroked himself. The softness of her fingers was so much more pleasurable than the feel of his own callused hands. Everything was better. Having her petite form nestled against his chest, the little moans she gave in the crook of his neck, the sheer decadence of the moment, everything contributed to making him lose his mind.

"Ah, yes..." The rest of the sentence was uttered in Norse, as he didn't want to shock her, but neither could he keep silent.

Make me come, you beauty, I'm about to burst. Watch me flood your hand, watch as I come for you.

As if she'd understood what he wanted, she drew away from him, so she could gaze at their entwined fingers and focus on what she was doing. Her lips parted on a gasp and it was his undoing. With a triumphant roar, he came, his seed shooting out of him with more force than it had ever done, coating both their hands in creamy release.

He collapsed, his knees weak, his back against the wall of the cave, his breath coming in short, ragged pants.

After a long moment, some clarity returned to his thoughts.

"I'm sorry. I shouldn't have done that." He shook his head, appalled. "I should have given you pleasure, not the other way around." That would have been a better way to distract her, and almost as satisfying.

But Agnes only smiled. "If we are talking about what we should or shouldn't have done, then I should probably not tell you this, but it did please me to do it. I have always been curious about the male body and the way it worked. And it is more fascinating that I could have imagined. You are a thing of wonder. Every part of you is."

He groaned. Did she have any idea what it would do to a man to hear that confession? He could still feel the aftermath of his release racing through his veins and she was praising his virility.

"Agnes. You're just too bloody perfect. I'm afraid I might consider bringing in a colony of bats to nest in the forge, if this is what you do when you need distracting from them." She bit her lower lip, not as amused by the jest as he had hoped. Of course she wasn't! What was the matter with him? She'd just told him she was scared of the beasts and here he was, threatening her with them. "Forgive me. I don't know why I said that."

But he knew exactly why. Because she had turned his body inside out, scrambled his brain and flipped his heart in his chest with a few strokes of her hand. There would be a before and after today, he could already feel it.

"It's all right. Only, my brothers did exactly that in our house when I was small, brought in a colony of bats. They locked me in with them. That is why I'm scared of them. It's silly, I know, as the bats didn't actually hurt me and were probably even more anxious to escape than I was, but I can't seem to help it."

Well, now he felt like the lowest of the low. As if that was not enough, he noticed the way she was surreptitiously trying to wipe her fingers on her skirt. Her perfect little fingers, which he had stained with his seed. Could he feel any worse?

"Please. Let me wash your hand. I came all over you."

She blushed a furious color at the unnecessary reminder. Really, did he have to be so blunt? Cursing himself for a fool, he pulled his braies back on and led Agnes to the mouth of the cave.

There was a rock just outside with a depression in it, which the storm had filled to the brim with rain. He plunged her hand into the cool water and started to brush each of her fingers in turn. His chest constricted. Had he ever handled anything more perfect than her soft, white hand? More beautiful? More fragile? The wrist was so slight, the nails so small, he barely dared touch her for fear of breaking her or damaging her.

"Forgive me, my hands are rough and I am not used to handling anything as delicate as your hands. I usually deal with hard metal."

For the first time in his life he regretted being a blacksmith. He felt like Skrýmir, the giant of his parents' stories, might do in front of humans. Hadn't Agnes already remarked on his bulk, if not exactly on his behavior? Wild, she'd called him. Well, he felt wild, compared to her.

She gave a small smile that breathed life back into his veins. She didn't seem mad at him at least. "I think you are underestimating yourself. I can hardly feel your touch. But I could have washed my hand myself. You didn't have to do that."

Of course he did. After soiling her with his release, cleaning her was the least he could do. He groaned.

What was wrong with him? He should have pushed her hand away before coming. But he could not have loosened the blessed grip around his cock if his life had depended on it. Thankfully, she had not seemed to take offense or recoiled in horror. She didn't even seem to mind having been used thus. It did little to lessen the guilt he felt, though.

"Please. Of course I did need to wash you. It's the least I can do."

Once she was clean, he wiped her fingers dry with the only part of himself that wasn't soaked, his undershirt. Agnes smiled her thanks then looked at the horizon and remarked, her voice expressionless. "The storm has passed, the rain has stopped."

Magnus stared at the sky. Indeed it had. He had not even noticed. "Yes."

But something else had just started.

CHAPTER SIX

The noises in the Norsemen village were different from the ones in her old village, and it always took Agnes a moment to remember where she was upon waking up. Then she recognized her new environment by the rhythmic *wooshing* of the windmill, the neighing of the horses, the guttural sounds of the Norse language. It was as different from the noises of her native place as if she had actually gone to a distant land.

But this morning it was different again. All she could hear were shouts and crackling sounds, the origin of which she could not identify. What was going on? And how had the unusual activity not woken her up before?

Because she'd been exhausted, that was why.

It had taken her a long time to fall asleep the night

before. Time and time again she had relived the moment when she had made Magnus explode in pleasure. It had been one of the most satisfying experiences in her life but now she was wondering. Would he not think her unforgivably brazen? Worse, would he now hope to use her in other ways? It would make sense for him to think that there was little harm in bedding a woman who had been so willing to offer him release when he'd not asked for anything. Would he turn into a lecher and pounce on her?

No, the man sleeping with his body curled up so protectively around her would never take advantage of her. He had promised he would not, and feminine instinct told her he would hold on to his promise. What had happened in the cave changed nothing.

Or at least, she hoped it did not. But the reality might not be so simple.

A spine-chilling scream had her shooting to her feet. What *was* going on this morning?

Agnes hastily put her dress on and walked out of the door, where she immediately understood the reason for the commotion. One of the huts over on the other side of the village was on fire. Dear God, what had happened? Were they under attack? Should she take a weapon? Thankfully, being a blacksmith, Magnus had plenty of instruments lying around. She grabbed a fearsome pair of pliers and headed straight out.

As she drew nearer to the crowd assembled by the mill, the roof of the hut gave out, and the whole thing collapsed on itself in a shower of sparks. Shock caused Agnes to skid to a halt. Dear God, had there been someone inside? As if in answer to her question, two men exited the cloud of smoke, holding a third one between them. Wolf and Sigurd, carrying Björn, whose clothes appeared singed. All three were coughing and stumbling but they were alive. She could only hope no one else was left to retrieve.

"What happened?" she asked a woman who was watching the events unfold with wide eyes.

"Dunne's hut caught fire earlier that morning. We don't know how it happened, as Dunne herself was not in. Thankfully, the men were able to contain the fire and it did not spread anywhere. And now that Björn is out, there will be no casualties either."

Agnes' heartbeat slowed down as relief spread through her. This was an accident, nothing more. The loss of the hut was a pity but no one had been hurt and no attackers were coming. She could relax.

Before she could ask any more questions Magnus appeared in front of her. Thankfully, he didn't seem to be injured.

"Are you all right?" she asked nonetheless. She needed to know he was not hurt.

"Yes. I will need a good wash though."

He rubbed at his red-rimmed eyes, which would be stinging badly because of the smoke, and looked at his body in consternation. Agnes could only agree he needed a wash. His hair was matted with sweat, his cheeks streaked with soot, his clothes filthy. It was all she could do not to gape. Clean, he was impressive enough. With black marks all over his skin, he was awe-inspiring, like a savage warrior on campaign.

"I'll go to the river now." Even his voice had gone rougher.

"Why don't you use the tub you found for me the other day? It should be big enough for you."

Three days ago Magnus had surprised her by hauling an enormous wooden basin into the forge, an old trough he'd cleaned and sanded. When she'd asked him about it, he'd replied that he wanted her to be able to wash with warm water. Unable to resist the offer, she had taken the first tub-bath of her life that very morning. The pleasure of lingering in warm water had been inde-scribable. She wasn't sure she would ever bear to wash in cold rivers ever again.

"It would be more comfortable and that way I will be able to help wash your hair and back."

The way Magnus stilled made her realize what she had just said. It had sounded so intimate, an offer only a wife would make. The woman she had been talking to gave a cough and hastened away, as embarrassed as if she and Magnus had started undressing one another in front of her.

"You would do that?" he asked, his eyes never leaving hers. She knew what he meant. After what had happened the day before, did she trust him not to overstep boundaries?

Yes, she did.

"I would."

Without a word he took her by the hand and led her to the forge. Even if she had wanted to retract her offer, she couldn't have. Her wild blacksmith was holding her too tightly.

EVEN WITH THE FIRE ROARING, it took forever, or so it seemed to Magnus, to heat up the bucket of water he'd placed at the center of the furnace. In the end, he didn't have the patience to wait until a second bucket was heated so he emptied the water he and Agnes had drawn from the well into the tub along with the hot one he'd just added. Cool water was better anyway. It might help him keep some control over his senses. Because he was fast regretting agreeing to her proposition. Well, not regretting it, but wondering how he was going to stop himself from demanding more than a wash once she put her perfect, wicked hands on him.

He hadn't been able to resist his need to be touched in the cave, when he'd been fully dressed, so what chances did he have now?

"Could you turn around while I get in the tub?" he asked, not sure why he was doing it. It was not as if he minded her seeing his naked body, or his hardness. It was not even as if it would be the first time she'd seen it. But she turned around without comment and busied herself with stoking the fire behind her.

When he was settled, with his legs dangling over the rim of the tub and his erection hidden under his cupped hands, he called out to her. "I'm ready."

Agnes moved so quietly he had not realized she'd come to the tub until he heard her voice in his ear.

"Shall we start with your back?"

He closed his eyes, as anticipation seared his every nerve ending.

Taking his silence for agreement, Agnes gathered his hair to place it over one shoulder, to give her access to his back. As she did so, her knuckles grazed his neck. A shiver descended all the way to his toes. She wet her hands before scooping some of the soap from the earthenware pot he'd brought from his hut. In a moment she would start. Then it would be too late. Perhaps it already was. He should have pointed out that he could wash on his own. He should have made her leave while she still could. But he merely nodded and bent forward to allow her to lather his shoulders and spine. When her hands, small and slick with soap, landed on his skin, he could not prevent another shiver. This was going to be torture.

And he would relish every moment of it.

As Agnes rubbed and circled his flesh, a groan built in his chest, and he could do nothing to stop it from escaping his lips. It came out like an animalistic snarl. The rhythm of her stroking faltered and he tensed in turn. Was she going to flee, frightened by his reaction?

Heart pounding, cock throbbing, he waited.

Eventually, she resumed her ministrations and he allowed himself to breathe again.

"What happened with the hut exactly? How did it catch on fire?"

That she was only asking to break through the tension of the moment was obvious, but he indulged her. Talking might help him keep the worst of his lust in check, and it was only normal that she should wonder what had happened.

"I'm not sure. All I know is that I saw the beginnings

of the fire while I was at the back of the forge. I called to a few men but we could not extinguish it. Dunne arrived when the flames had already spread to the roof. The hut was beyond saving at that point, so she urged us not to put ourselves in danger. We simply ensured the fire did not spread to the other huts, or even more importantly, the mill. Fortunately, it was not a windy day."

It would have been a disaster otherwise.

"But if she didn't want anyone to try and save the hut, how did Björn end up trapped inside?" Agnes asked, moving the wet hair to his other shoulder.

"Because all of a sudden Dunne's daughter ran into the inferno, crying that she wanted to save her cat." Magnus remembered the horror on everyone's face when Dawn had escaped her mother's grasp. There had been no need to do anything, however, because Björn had moved before anyone else could react. Quick as a flash, he'd rushed after the little girl. The door had collapsed just after him, blocking their retreat. For a moment it had looked as if all was lost.

The hands at his back stopped and he heard an intake of breath. "She didn't!"

"I'm afraid she did, but Björn was able to lift her out of the window. Both of them are well, as is the cat," he reassured her. "Wolf and Sigurd hacked a hole through the wall just in time to get Björn out."

Silence followed his declaration. Then slender fingers slid down his spine, before stopping just above the water surface, and dangerously close to his loins.

"Shall I continue?" Agnes rasped when he didn't react.

Yes. *No!* Please.

"I... I think it might be better to use a cloth to rub at my face and hands," he said in lieu of an answer. "The soot will come more easily that way."

That, and the fact that he could not imagine feeling her bare hands gliding over his chest. Because this time, she would be facing him and she would see the hunger in his eyes. He was too weak to put an end to the moment, but he could at least put a barrier between their skins, flimsy as it was.

"You're right, I should have thought." Agnes sounded as breathless as he was. "Let me go get one from your hut."

Alone in the rapidly cooling water, Magnus tried to calm down the beating of his heart. Or rather, the pulsing in his groin. That was as excruciating, as delicious as he had feared. What had possessed him to accept Agnes' offer? Come to that, what had possessed her to offer such an intimate thing as to wash him? The woman was full of surprises. Shy as she appeared at first glance, she had agreed to his suggestion that they should sleep next to one another mere days after having met him. In the cave, she had behaved with the most disconcerting brazenness, even though she had been new to such caresses. And now she was running her hands all over his body as if it were the normal thing to do. Didn't she know where this could end?

Where it *would* end if he had his say?

No. It wouldn't lead anywhere. Officially, he was here to wash the soot away, and that was all he would do if it killed him. She had washed the only part of his body he didn't have access to. The rest, he could bloody well wash by himself, starting with his hair. He could not risk having her hands anywhere near his throbbing member, because then he would lose his mind and make her do what he had already made her do back in the cave, when he should have asked why she was afraid of bats instead of using her to slake the lust raging in his blood. Anything but that.

One moment of folly might be forgiven, two would establish him as a despicable lecher who thought nothing of using innocent women for his selfish pleasure.

That sealed it. When she came back with the cloth, he would tell her he would finish washing on his own. Nothing would happen today.

With decision, he plunged his soapy head under the water.

Agnes clutched the piece of cloth tight against her chest as if by doing so she could prevent her heart from exploding. Touching Magnus' back, even if she had tried to keep her gestures brisk and efficient, had been heavenly. His skin had been so smooth, the muscles underneath so taut, vibrant with power. How would she cope with touching the rest of him?

With touching the part she had already stroked once and was desperate to stroke again? She had not missed how he had kept his hands in his lap while she washed him, so as to hide his member from view.

Had he been hard? Had he simply wanted to avoid her seeing anything she wasn't supposed to see? She had been unable to think of anything else until she'd asked him about the fire.

Shouldn't she give him the cloth and leave him to finish his bath alone? Yes. Would she be able to? She wasn't sure. In any case, she needed to go now. She could not leave him to wait for her indefinitely.

When she entered the forge again, Agnes thought for a moment that Magnus had finished his ablutions without her and left. It would make sense, considering how long she had taken to build up the courage to get back to him. The water would be cold by now, and who liked to linger in a too small, no longer warm tub? Then she saw the long legs draped over the rim. No wonder she had not seen his head and neck. They were submerged under water. Dread spiked through her, like hundreds of ice shards piercing her skin all at once. Had he fallen asleep and drowned while she was getting the cloth? Dear God, no!

She rushed to him, hoping not to be too late.

"Magnus!"

Kneeling on the floor, she put her hands into the water to lift him up. At the exact same time, he resurfaced of his own accord. What happened next was inevitable.

Their lips met, his warm and wet from the water, hers cold and stiff from the fear she had just experienced.

It was not a kiss, precisely, more an accidental collision of lips, but she knew instantly it would become a kiss. And maybe more. As soon as they touched, she was seized by the irresistible urge to let Magnus take what he wanted from her.

And take it he did.

Thinking she deserved to experience at least some of the things men and women could share together, even if she didn't mean to marry, Agnes had kissed a boy from her village some years ago, and it had been nice enough. This was not nice. It was hot, it was fiery, it was scandalous, it was... well, like Magnus himself, wild.

The relief of knowing he had not drowned, the pleasure his touch created within her, the thrill of being in the proximity of a naked man, everything conspired to make her melt.

His wet hands grabbed the back of her neck at the same time as he raised himself up to a sitting up position in order to devour her more fully. She moaned, and had to place her palms on his slippery shoulders to steady herself. The kiss deepened, and he started to use his tongue was well as his lips, massaging hers, transforming her into a liquid mass of limbs. She felt as if she were floating in a tub of warm water herself.

"Agnes—"

"I thought you'd drowned," she cried out as soon as he freed her mouth.

"I didn't. But we shouldn't—"

She cut him short by deepening the kiss even further, bringing her teeth into it to nibble at his lower lip. She didn't want to hear he regretted kissing her, she especially didn't want to hear that they should stop. Because she most decidedly disagreed. They should carry on. For a moment she thought she'd won. He seemed to surrender, and tightened his hold over the back of her neck. Then he wrenched himself away from her with a grunt that could have been one of despair or frustration.

"Wait, Agnes," he said again, holding her at arms' length. No matter how much she wanted to, there was no way she would manage to come closer now. He was just too strong.

"Magnus," was all she could answer.

"If you don't stop, I will do something I'm not sure you want me to do."

Right this moment she could not think of a single thing he could do to her that wouldn't be welcomed, but she knew to what he was referring. "Like yesterday in the cave you mean?" she breathed.

His blue eyes caught fire. "No. Nothing like that. In the cave you gave me pleasure. It was all about me. Today it would be all about you. If you don't go now, I will put my hands on you, my face and my mouth and my tongue between your legs. I will devour you. I won't stop until I've seen you explode in release, heard you scream my name and made you beg for more. You're a woman, you can give me your pleasure over and over again. And I will make you do it, whether you want it or not."

It was a good thing Agnes was already kneeling, because she might well have dissolved to the floor in a puddle of need otherwise.

Today it would be all about you. I will devour you.

How did he think that she wouldn't want that?

Perhaps she was not supposed to feel this way, but how could she stop herself? Had he threatened to take her, she might have taken fright. But he had not. He had talked about pleasuring her with his hands, his mouth, his tongue. None of these could make her with child so she had nothing to fear. And with fear gone, all that was left was desire.

The desire to feel what other women allowed themselves to feel when they wanted a man.

With other men, resisting the temptation had not been an issue. They had not stirred her, whether in body or in soul, so it had been easy to stick to her resolve not to let anyone get too close to her physically, much less emotionally.

With Magnus... With him everything was different. New. Exciting.

Scary.

She felt ill-equipped to face it, or even simply make sense of it. It was hard to understand why that might be. Or maybe it was not so hard. The blacksmith was not only shockingly handsome, but he was also unlike any of the men she had met, or more pointedly, he was unlike the men she had known all her life. How could she have felt any attraction toward friends she had seen covered in mud a dozen times? There was nothing enticing about someone she still remembered as a pimply youth. As to wanting to kiss someone she'd seen kiss all her friends in turn, it was unthinkable.

But she had only met Magnus as a grown woman, he didn't have a single pimple on his face, he had not kissed anyone she knew, and they had never fallen into a bog together. He was also a Norseman, as different from what she knew as could be conceived. No wonder she was intrigued.

More than intrigued.

And so now she wondered if she had not made a mistake in going so far from her village. The familiar environment was exactly what she needed to help her keep her unwise impulses on a tight leash. Here, away from all she knew, left to her own device, she was afraid her inner demons would run riot.

How was she going to resist what she felt when nothing or no one was here to stop her?

Alone in a new place, in a handsome stranger's house, she felt as vulnerable as a solitary flame struggling to burn bright once it had been taken out into the wind blowing outside. How long would she be able to resist in the new conditions? She might well be destroyed. Yes... Except she had now met a man who made his living from fanning flames and transforming them into infernos hot enough to melt metal. He did not destroy fire, he mastered it. Under his expert coaxing, the little fragile flame she was had the potential to grow invincible. It was an irresistible thought.

"You need to go now, Agnes, because I'm telling you, you do not know what you're dealing with. I'm a hair's breadth from taking what I want from you, and it is more than you are prepared to give, this much I can guarantee."

"I'm not afraid of you."

"You should be."

"Of you? Never."

This was not in question. She had seen enough of him to know that, contrary to what he thought, he would never force her to do anything she didn't want to do. He would never take more than she was prepared to give. No, if she was afraid, and admittedly, right now, she was, it was of her, of her inability to stick to her resolve never to get close to a man.

All of a sudden he stood up in a rush of sluicing water. Overawed, Agnes watched the man standing proud in front of her. The Norse god, she should perhaps say. On his broad shoulders his wet hair traced intricate patterns. She could not help but stare at them. It was like a secret message etched on his bare skin, written only for her. But what was it telling her?

Keep out?

Or *come here if you dare?*

Dare she?

She allowed her gaze to wander over him. Every inch of his body was sheer masculine perfection, from the strong chest and flat stomach to the proud length jutting between the two thickest thighs she had ever seen. My... Wild did not begin to describe him. By comparison she felt as fragile as a kitten.

"This is me," he said, gesturing at himself. "Still unafraid? Still sure you could take me in all my potency? Be careful. I work with fire and I don't want you to get burned. I feel I might be just as dangerous to you as my furnace is to me."

"You are not dangerous." Hadn't she just been thinking he knew how to handle fire, tame it even? She had nothing to fear from him.

"Right now that's exactly now I feel. You know what I'm capable of, what I made you do in that cave. It is nothing compared to what I want to make you do now."

As if to illustrate the point, he gave a growl deep in his throat. In that moment he looked more than wild, he looked just as he'd said, dangerous. Not to her physical integrity, she was still convinced he would not hurt her, but to her heart. She might trust he would not damage her bodily envelope but she was not so certain he would not reach what was hidden inside her, the soft parts she had never exposed to the world. With him, those parts were not as well-protected as she'd wished, as they'd been so far.

Because she was small and shy, people assumed she had no backbone. The opposite was actually true. Unassuming as she was, Agnes was all backbone, she'd had to be, because there had been no other choice, no one else would have looked after her. But after years of strain, her protection had become brittle. It felt as if might snap at any moment. It should have worried her, and it did. But perhaps it needn't do. Hadn't she just met a blacksmith equipped with all the tools needed to forge her a new one if need be?

Magnus might be the only man capable both of shattering the determination holding her upright and then putting her back together even stronger than before.

Happier.

He wrapped a hand around the rod that had shown no sign of flagging during their discussion. The gesture was at once crude, frightening, and arousing as hell. Under her fascinated gaze, he started to stroke himself.

"Agnes. See what you do to me. You drive me mad." The voice was raw, and the strokes soon became punishing. This was nothing like the timid caresses she had given him in the cave. Unable to look away, she stared, willing him to bring his pleasure in the manner he was used to, suspecting it would be much more satisfying to watch than when she had done it. This would be uncompromisingly masculine. Perfect. A grunt escaped his lips and he threw his head back, breaking eye contact. The muscles and sinews on his neck twisted and corded, betraying immense strength.

Agnes forgot to breathe.

"Go, now, or I swear I'll—"

There was such anguish in his voice that this time she took fright. He was no longer worried for her, but for his own sanity.

Not waiting until he erupted, she turned and fled.

CHAPTER SEVEN

That night, Magnus pretended he had a sword to finish and spent the night at the forge. He doubted Agnes had swallowed the lie but it mattered not. The important thing was that it allowed him to stay away from her and the pallet they had shared for two nights. He could not risk a repeat of the afternoon's events, when he had frightened poor Agnes to death, first by making her think he'd drowned, then by threatening to eat her whole and finally by stroking himself in front of her with unrestrained ferocity. The release he had forced out of his overstrung body once she'd left had caused him to collapse to his knees in the icy water.

After an agitated night, he was up at the crack of dawn, as usual. Though he was famished, he didn't dare go back home in case he saw Agnes. He feared seeing the condemnation in her eyes, he feared even more seeing desire because he would not be able to resist it. He would tumble her into the pallet and caution be damned. So instead he went to Wolf's hut. The Icelander would be up as well and, in exchange for a piece of bread and some cheese, Magnus would offer to help him with the fence. It was the best solution for now.

As he'd expected, his friend was only too glad to accept his help.

"Steinar and Torsten have become veritable terrors. I need something to stop them from destroying our vegetables and terrorizing the chickens," he told Magnus, the softening in his eyes at the mention of his sons belying the words. Despite the boys' undeniable boisterousness, he would not be without them for the world. "And seeing as Merewen is going to give me another little scamp in the new year, I'd better take my precautions now."

Magnus slapped him on the shoulder. He hadn't known about this new pregnancy and he was delighted for his friend. "Congratulations."

"Thank you, even though in truth, you have no reason to congratulate me. My part in the whole affair was easy, and more pleasurable than words can express. Merewen will be the one doing the hard part." A shadow passed over the Icelander's face. The birth of his second son had been difficult and it had taken his wife a while to recover from it. Wolf had been nothing like his usual self during the long weeks she'd spent lying in bed, building up her strength again. "I wish such joy for me did not come at such a high price for her."

Magnus didn't have any children, but he thought he understood what his friend meant exactly. Men were powerless when it came to childbirth. All their supposed physical superiority counted for nothing. Women were the ones possessed with the true force. They alone gave life, their babies were literally wrenched from their bodies. As Wolf said, men's part in the process was pitiful. They could only watch and try not to go mad when the women they loved suffered agony. Not to mention that a happy deliverance could not be guaranteed.

All in all, a birth was a tense moment, and he could understand his friend's ambivalent feelings.

"Come," he told him. "Let us ensure the food needed to feed your family this winter is not destroyed by two little blond monsters. That much, at least, we can do."

It took them all morning to finish the fence but by the end of it, Magnus was confident even a charging bull would not have presented any threat to it. The chickens and the leeks were safe from Steinar and Torsten. After partaking of a hearty stew prepared by Merewen, he decided to go and see Björn. He was only stalling, and he knew he would eventually have to go back home and face Agnes, but he could not bring himself to do it just yet. Besides, he wanted to see how his friend fared after his ordeal of the previous day.

To his surprise, he found him in bed. That was unlike him. Björn was more active than most. Had he been more seriously injured than he'd thought?

"How are you doing?" Magnus asked, sitting on the stool by the pallet where his bare-chested friend lay. There was a bandage wrapped around his left bicep and the skin above it appeared burned but, as far as he could see, that was the extent of the damage. He'd been lucky. And yet he was grimacing, like a man in pain.

"I'm fine."

He didn't look fine. He didn't even sound fine. "I've never seen you lying in bed during the day. You cannot be fine."

"I'm fine," Björn repeated, a hint of irritation creeping in his voice. "Only, I have no reason to get up, so I didn't."

No reason? What an odd thing to say. Since when did people need reasons to get up? It was what you did in the morning, you didn't question it. "What about—"

"You don't look too well either, if I may say," his

friend interrupted. "What is the matter with you? Why aren't you at the forge in the middle of the day?"

Because everything had been turned on its head, that was why, and in the forge was a woman he didn't know what to make of. Or rather, he knew all too well. Only, he wasn't sure she was ready for it. Or willing. And so he avoided the place.

Magnus sagged on the stool. Suddenly he understood what his friend meant by not having a reason not to get up. He never asked himself why he was getting up in the morning, because he feared the answer would depress him, and he always went to bed dissatisfied with his day, which was an even more worrying situation.

"My life is a waste," he said instead of answering. "I'm thirty summers and I don't know what I'm doing, or what I want. Can you think of anything worse?"

"Oh yes, I can." Björn twisted his lips. "Worse than not knowing what you want is knowing exactly what you want and being unable to get it."

Magnus gave this some consideration and decided that yes, it might well be worse. "What is this thing you want and cannot have then?"

"A woman." The two words were little more than a breath.

Magnus arched a brow. A woman? He'd never seen his friend with anyone, so the answer surprised him.

Björn had never even seemed interested in women, yet he was saying that what he needed to make his life complete was a woman. He had not seen that coming. But that was hardly an issue, because Magnus didn't doubt the man could have all the women he wanted. He was handsome, personable and trustworthy.

"You're still young, you've got your whole life ahead of you to—"

"Will you all just stop referring to my age! I'm plenty old enough to know my own mind and crave a family." He gave a sigh, as if he hadn't meant to snarl. "But I don't want just any woman. That's the trouble."

Oh, so he had his eye set on someone who didn't want him. That was undoubtedly a complication. Magnus should know, he who had never managed to make anyone want him.

"Who is she?"

Silence was his only answer, then Björn threw an involuntary glance at the bandage on his bicep. Everything became clear.

"Frigyth's sister, Dunne?"

Of course, *she* was the reason the man had run into the burning hut to save Dawn. Magnus had wondered what had possessed the man to act so quickly, as if his life rather than that of the little girl's depended on him saving her.

"Yes. Dunne. It's always been her for me, ever since I first saw her all those years ago." Björn gave a smile that resembled a scowl. "But unfortunately, she doesn't feel the same about me. When we saw that her hut was burning I was asking her to marry me, believe it or not. She refused."

"And still you risked your life to save her daughter?"

The look Björn threw him would have doused the flames in his furnace as efficiently as a bucket of ice-cold water. "Are you suggesting we should have let her burn?"

"No. Of course not. Forgive me, I didn't mean to suggest anything of the sort. Apparently, it is not only my life that is a mess. My mind is also addled."

Magnus shook his head. Had he really asked that stupid question? Yes. As he'd said, his mind must seriously be addled. Fortunately, Björn didn't seem to really think the worst of him. He merely nodded.

"I would have gone to rescue any poor child trapped in a burning hut. But I would not have felt the agony I felt when I saw it was Dunne's daughter who was in danger. Because her pain is my pain. And I would like her joys to be my joys for the rest of our lives. Only she doesn't want to share them with me." Björn hid his eyes with a bent arm, like a man weary beyond measure. "And so now you know why I have no reason to get up."

Magnus swallowed.

Her pain is my pain. And I would like her joys to be my joys.

Yes, that was a good way of expressing what he felt about Agnes.

He'd thought he wanted her body, and he did. He'd thought he wanted to keep her safe, and he did. But he also wanted more. He wanted what Björn wanted with Dunne. Dunne, who for a reason he was ignorant of, had refused the offer of marriage she'd received. Would he, Magnus, have more luck when he proposed to the woman of his dreams? He started as the thought crossed his mind. Was he really considering marrying Agnes? Was he really about to risk another humiliation, like the one he had suffered at Edith's hands, and ask if she would have him?

He shot to his feet. Yes, he was. Because there was no better way to keep her with him always.

This conversation had been most illuminating.

"I think actually I do know what I want to do with my life," he said, talking almost to himself. He wanted to spend it with Agnes.

Björn opened one eye. The ghost of a smile flickered across his lips. "Well, then, my friend, go tell her."

THAT VERY AFTERNOON, under the pretense of showing her how he threw stones, Magnus took Agnes to the clearing in the forest. As she had asked a few times if he could show her how he hunted birds, she didn't think anything of the request and followed him without comment.

It was time to address what was simmering between them. Because there was something, it was undeniable, a connection such as he'd never felt with anyone before. And unless he was mistaken, Agnes felt it, too. As he'd told Björn, he was thirty summers, a man grown, it was high time his life acquired a purpose.

Their conversation had opened his eyes. The man had almost died saving the daughter of the woman he loved and would do so again if need be. When Wolf and Sigurd had carried his limp form to the bed, coughing, and spluttering, Dunne was all he had talked about. His voice hoarse from having spent too long inhaling smoke, his eyes weeping, his body burned and covered in soot, he'd repeated her name over and over again, asking them if she was all right, even though he was the injured one.

Magnus was suddenly seized by the certainty that Agnes' name would be the first and only word on his lips if he ever escaped death like Björn had just done. He would not worry about himself, but about never seeing her again. And because of that, he knew he had to ask the question that had been burning his lips ever since he'd left Björn's hut. The question he'd not thought to ask any woman ever again.

Well, he had to, because his life, already largely meaningless, would not be worth living until he'd had an answer. Sven was convinced the two of them were involved? It was time to make it happen.

"What type of stones do you use?" Agnes asked, her voice as calm as usual. "Big ones, I imagine?"

His chest constricted. Perhaps he was wrong, and she didn't feel any tension between them. If he didn't know better, he might think she had forgotten what had happened yesterday. She appeared unperturbed. Looking around as if in search of a suitable pebble, she bent down and picked one the size of an egg. A good choice, he had to admit, but his mind was not on the task at hand. He was too busy watching her and building up the courage to speak his mind to worry about the best projectile to fell birds.

"One like this?"

With a smile she deposited the stone into his open palm. Before he could think, he dropped it on the ground and took her hand instead.

"Agnes. I have a question to ask. I hope it will not take you by surprise, after what we did yesterday."

After they'd kissed, he meant. Had she felt what he

had felt when their lips had worshipped each other's? Had she seen the inevitability of it? He could only hope so.

Gathering all his courage, he fell to his knees.

"What are you doing?"

She sounded, and looked flustered. A good sign? He didn't give himself time to think about it, for fear of seeing his strength desert him.

"Will you marry me?"

Silence descended into the clearing. The wind stilled, the leaves in the trees stopped rustling. Even the birds seemed to suspend their chirping for a moment. Her hand still clasped in his, Agnes was immobile as a statue. There was no need to wait for her answer to know she was about to refuse. She had paled so much one would have thought he'd just asked if he could hack her to pieces, like a real Norse invader.

"I see. You won't," he said flatly, getting back to his feet. There was no point in waiting for an answer that would be negative. There was a limit to what a man was prepared to endure. Why oh why had he thought this would go better than it had gone with Edith? Would he ever learn? People did not want him, women would not commit to him. They allowed him to bed them, but nothing more. They wanted pleasure, protection and material advantages, but not a lifetime by his side.

"I'm sorry, Magnus, but I-I can't marry you."

Though that was not quite what he had expected her to say, it didn't make it any better. It was still a refusal. "Why not?"

Her eyes filled with tears and, for a moment, he thought she would throw herself into his arms. His body tensed in preparation for the impact. It never came.

"I'm sorry."

With those words, she turned and fled, just like she had the day before. Only this time, he had not ordered her to go, she had decided all on her own that she could not stay a moment longer with him.

He did pick up the egg-shaped stone then, and threw it as far as he could, letting out a grunt of anger as he let it fly. Another stone was flung, then another, and another. Far from helping, each target he hit increased his frustration. Aye, he could throw stones and hit his mark every time, but what good did that do? The skill was useless, *he* was useless, and Agnes did not want him.

A dead branch on the nearest tree came crashing down when he aimed a fist-sized stone at it. Of course she did not want him, why would she, no one ever did. A piece of rock split in half when he hit it with a pointy pebble. She cared nothing for him, just like everyone else. An empty bird's nest was knocked off its perch when he threw a heavy stone at it.

His last projectile embedded itself into a young sapling's bark, inflicting a wound not dissimilar to the one Agnes had just inflicted on his heart. Yes, on his heart, not his pride, which was far, far worse.

He fell to his knees.

CHAPTER EIGHT

It did not surprise Magnus to see that Agnes' meagre possessions had been removed by the time he got back home that night. After refusing his offer of marriage, she would have felt uncomfortable sleeping in his hut. In his bed.

In his arms.

He told himself it was for the best, as he might have begged her to reconsider her answer if he'd seen her and the last thing he needed was to make a fool of himself.

Where had she gone? He didn't think she would have left the village, not this late in the day. At least he hoped she had not. Traveling alone at night was too dangerous for a woman on her own. He forced himself to calm. Agnes was sensible, not prone to inconsiderate actions, so she would have known not to attempt such folly. Perhaps she was with Ingrid. The two of them had become very close in a short time.

Yes, he reflected bitterly, but sometimes, a few days were all the time you needed to know who mattered to you. He'd not known her for longer than Ingrid had and yet it had been enough to convince him she could be the one giving meaning to his life.

As soon as he lay down on the pallet her scent hit him, reminding him she had spent a few nights by his side and could have spent many more had she accepted his offer of marriage. With a cry of rage he stood up and hurled the furs against the door. The soft material did not make for a satisfying impact so he sent the earthenware pitcher crashing against the wall instead, where it splintered in a thousand pieces. Much better. His mood darker than it had ever been, Magnus stormed to the forge, where he settled for the night in the back room. The cloth on the pallet smelled of male sweat, courtesy of Sven's recent visit. Not ideal, but anything was better than being bathed in Agnes' floral bouquet.

He did *not* want to dream of her.

The next day he did not get out of bed. With no small amount of derision, he reflected that he now understood what Björn had meant about having no reason to get up. For the first time in his life he remained where he was, only getting up to see to his needs and grab a loaf of bread he ate while staring at the ceiling.

The following morning, he forced himself to get up. He refused to become an even more pathetic figure than he already was. And perhaps if he behaved as he normally did, eventually he would heal.

One could only hope.

He started as he did every day, by stoking his furnace. It should have been the work of a moment, but for the first time since he'd taken over the forge, the flames refused to cooperate. What an apt, if dispiriting image that was. He was coaxing the fire back to life in the same way he was trying to breathe some life into his empty soul by pretending everything was normal.

He pressed on the bellows with a new determination. He might not be able to force Agnes or anyone to be with him, but he could bloody well make some wood catch on fire as it was supposed to.

Once he'd finally imposed his will on the stubborn flames, Sigurd's wife Frigyth walked into the forge, her face wreathed in smiles. His own mood darkened further. How could anyone be happy right now? Though it was a gorgeous sunny day, it seemed to him that everything was grey. In a hope to pound some of the frustration and misery out of him, he'd decided to start on the gate that had been commissioned the day before

Agnes' arrival. In normal circumstances he would have relished the challenging the task represented, but after meeting her, he had lacked the motivation and the time for such a major undertaking. In the evening he'd only wanted to rush out of the forge and be with her. Well, he had time now, and he badly needed to hit at something.

If he completed the gate, at least one good thing might come out of this whole mess.

"Good morning, Magnus," Frigyth said, ignoring the grunt he'd given her as a greeting.

"Did Sigurd send you to get his nails? I'm sorry, they're not quite ready yet." Damnation, he'd only just remembered about that particular commission. Really, where had his mind gone? The answer hit him square in the chest. To the woman who'd stolen his heart.

"No. I came to invite you to a wedding."

A wedding?

He almost dropped the piece of metal from his tongs. Were the gods intent on torturing him, aided by a petite, friendly Saxon? He didn't want to hear about weddings right now, when he'd only just been forced to accept that *he* would never get anyone to agree to marry him. Could this day get any worse? The last thing he needed to make his humiliation complete was for Sven to walk into the room and announce that he'd happened to be in the clearing the day before and had heard Agnes refuse him.

For the first time in his life, he might well punch his brother.

"Who's getting married then?" he growled, thinking back to how Agnes had once called him wild. Right now, he felt positively feral. In truth he didn't care about the wedding, but he had to say something.

"Björn and my sister." Frigyth laughed. "I don't think it will surprise you."

"No," he said, since that was obviously what was expected of him. But it did surprise him. Hadn't Björn told him only the day before that the Saxon had refused his offer of marriage? Apparently, she had changed her mind.

He sighed. It seemed that Björn was about to get his dearest wish granted. Magnus did not begrudge the man his happiness but all the same, his guts felt as if he'd been forced to swallow a dozen of his sharpest nails. Was he the only one destined to be left behind?

"So, can you come this afternoon?" Frigyth looked at him curiously, as if she'd understood what he was thinking about.

"This afternoon?" My, that was quick work. There was only one explanation for the haste. The woman had been head over heels in love with Björn all the time as well and had only refused him for a reason that had nothing to do with him. Women. Did they enjoy torturing men?

"Yes. They don't want to wait another moment."

Magnus sighed again and threw his hammer on the workbench, utterly defeated. He wouldn't be making a gate today either. It seemed he'd been right, and the gods *were* conspiring against him.

"Yes. Of course I will be there."

Not to see Agnes, he told himself sternly, but because more than ever, he needed to feel he was part of the community. After all, it was the only way to guarantee he did not end up all alone.

Seeing the love in Björn and Dunne's eyes as they exchanged their vows would have made everyone cry, Agnes told herself to justify the need to wipe at her eyes. It seemed that, with the right man, marriage did not have to be the prison she had always likened it to. She had no doubt Björn would do nothing to cause his new wife a moment's displeasure. He would be an attentive husband, and a loving father, nothing like her own had been. Not only would he not mind Dunne bearing him girls, but before the ceremony he had adopted Dawn, the daughter she'd had from her previous union, with as much enthusiasm as if she had been born of his loins.

The new family would be happy together, that was certain.

Agnes made her way to village square, and the banquet awaiting them, in a pensive mood. Her lifelong convictions had taken a serious beating this afternoon and she wasn't sure how to recover.

Once the feast was over and the couples started dancing, Ingrid came to find her, a wistful expression on her face. She sat down on the stool next to her and sighed.

"My big brother married. I can't believe it." She sounded rather emotional, and perhaps slightly tipsy after having indulged in a healthy dose of mead during the meal. Linking arms with her, she placed her head over her shoulder. "I wish our parents had been here to see this."

Agnes knew the two Danes had recently died in a tragic accident so she could only agree. "They would have been happy to see their son marry the love of his life."

Because that was what was happening. It had not taken her long to understand that the real reason Björn had refused her father's suggestion that the two of them marry was that he was in love with another Saxon woman. He'd told her his refusal had nothing to do with her, and he hadn't lied. It had been motivated by his desire to be with Dunne.

"Yes, I have no doubt he'll be happy with Dunne, and her little girl," Ingrid said on another sigh. "Apparently, he's only ever had eyes for her, ever since they met four years ago. Oh, forgive me, I shouldn't have said that."

"Why not?" It was true. Anyone could see the two of them were meant for each other, even if Dunne had fought the evidence at first.

"Because I know you were hoping to marry Björn. And I'll admit I wanted you to as well." She made a face. "We would have been sisters then, not just friends. It would have been perfect. We get on so well, don't you think?"

They did, but Agnes had to rectify her friend's impression. She had never hoped to marry Björn. Her father had wanted to force him into the match for his own benefit, which was not the same at all. But the Norseman had told her in no uncertain terms he would not agree to it. It was true Agnes had felt the sting of rejection at first, because she had not known his feelings for Dunne at the time. The thought had crossed her mind that if she had to marry against her will, she could do worse than Björn, who was not only stunning to look at but protective and kind as well. Such a man would have made a good husband for anyone, and she might have been able to conquer her fears for him.

However, she had quickly seen that his heart only belonged to one woman, and that woman was not her. It had simply not been meant to be, and had only comforted her in the notion that marriage was not for her.

"That's not quite what I—"

The words dried on Agnes' lips when she spotted Magnus standing at the end of the table, a tankard of ale in his hand. He was staring at her, his eyes ablaze with such fury that it reminded her of the fire he stoked every morning in his forge. How she had missed him the last two nights! Waking up alone and cold had made her see what her existence would be like on her own. True, she wouldn't have to worry about her health or fear bad treatment if she never married, but she wouldn't feel any joy either, she wouldn't have anything to look forward to when she woke up in the morning and no one to cuddle up next to at night.

At the moment, it seemed like a bad bargain.

Watching Magnus at his work, making him laugh, nestling into his warmth as they lay together in bed had been simple pleasures she was not sure she could do without.

It had broken her heart to refuse his offer, and possibly also his. Up until then she had not thought he would, or could, return her budding feelings for him. But it seemed she had been wrong. The look in his eyes when she had refused him had been caused by more than bruised pride.

Was that why he was glowering at her right now? Because he was remembering the pain she had caused him? Unfortunately, it might well be. She had been rather blunt, and had fled before she'd offered him any explanation. Then blood froze in her veins when she realized there was another explanation for his anger. He had heard what Ingrid had said. And he now thought she was in love with Björn and had been hoping to marry him. He would think that was why she had refused his offer of marriage the other day, because she had her eyes set on someone else.

Her stomach dropped to the soles of her feet. This was not the impression she wanted to give, because it was not true. She didn't want anyone else, never had, and possibly never would. The only man she would consider marrying was looking at her as he would to an enemy.

She stood up, intent on setting the record straight. They could not part on a misunderstanding. "Magnus—"

Before she could say anything, he slammed the tankard on the table and stormed in the direction of the forge.

"Will you excuse me?" Agnes shouted to Ingrid, who was asking what could possibly require her attention when they were in the middle of a conversation. But she didn't have time to answer the question.

She had a furious blacksmith to soothe.

CHAPTER NINE

The door of the forge opened without a sound. Only the burst of moonlight painting the room in bluish hues betrayed the fact that someone had slipped inside. Someone too small and dainty to make any noise on the packed earth floor. Someone who had not set foot in here for two days. In other words, an eternity.

Magnus didn't move, and the door closed again, wrapping the room in shadows once more. To the left, the faint glow of the embers cut through the darkness, like the many eyes of a malevolent creature intent on witnessing the humiliation that was sure to come. What was Agnes doing here? Hadn't she done enough?

After a moment, her voice reached him, oddly

disembodied. "Magnus? I know you're in here. Please, we need to talk. I owe you an explanation."

An explanation! He was in no mood to hear why she thought Björn was better than him.

"You owe me nothing," he growled.

Damnation, he had not meant to talk at all. Now not only Agnes would know for sure that he was here, but also where he was standing.

Having located him she started to walk up in his direction, stumbling a little. Her eyes would not have adjusted to the obscurity yet, unlike his. Magnus braced himself for the moment she would fall to her knees or flat on her face. Hadn't she told him she was clumsy? Perhaps she'd been right to make the claim, because she appeared particularly unsteady. But she made it to him without any mishap, stopping close enough for him to see her eyes glitter like liquid gems.

"Please, you must—"

"Why are you here?" he cut in, annoyed at her insistence, annoyed even more by his weakness. He should not want to lift her into his arms, he should not be hoping to hear that she had changed her mind, like Dunne had done about Björn's offer. He should refuse to listen to her and storm out. "Have you come to beg me to have you now that the possibility of marrying the man you wanted is gone? How many times did you make him come like you did me since you arrived in the village? Well, whatever you did, it was all for nothing, for the only woman he wants is Dunne,"

It was a low blow, but he could not help himself. Her rejection had hurt too deeply for him to be reasonable. How had he not guessed that she had refused him because she was in love with another man, a man she could never have, because he would only ever have eyes for the woman he had married this afternoon? He should have relished her suffering, thinking it just retribution for the pain and humiliation she had inflicted on him, but, like the fool he was, he felt nothing but sympathy. He knew all too well how painful it was to be left behind by people you loved and he could not wish the agony on anyone, much less the woman standing in front of him.

"I've never made Björn or anyone else come, only you." She sounded hurt rather than outraged at the suggestion, as if she had hoped better from him. For a long moment she stayed silent, then she straightened to her full height, as if she'd taken a decision. He tensed up in turn. Finally they would get to the heart of the matter. "I'm here to tell you that Ingrid is mistaken. I never wanted Björn. I want you. No one else."

Everything within him surged.

I want you. No one else.

The very words he had never heard in his life, and

always hankered after. Could he dare to hope she meant them, and everything would be all right? No. Not yet. Being too hasty had gotten him in all sorts of trouble. He needed to understand, ensure he was not making another mistake.

"You want me, yet you refused to marry me." It made no sense. But hadn't Dunne refused Björn's offer of marriage a few days ago? And now they were husband and wife. Perhaps there was no accounting for what went on in a woman's mind.

"Yes. I told you I could not marry you, not that I did not want to."

Brow furrowed, he realized she was right. She had said "I can't marry you" not "I don't want to". Why not? What was there to stop her? Was she already married? Was that why she had left her village at the first opportunity? To flee a husband she didn't love? It was not impossible. Björn had told him she was fleeing something.

There was an ominous silence. Even as the thought crossed his mind, Magnus wondered how a silence could be ominous.

Like this, his fevered mind told him. *Exactly like this.*

Heart drumming in his chest, he waited.

When Agnes started talking, she did so in a flat voice that tugged at his heart. "My mother married a man she didn't love at a young age and bore him ten children. She lost three of the babes, and almost died giving birth to the last one, when I was seven years old. She died earlier this year, still young. I have no doubt all the pregnancies brought her to an early grave."

"I'm sorry," Magnus said inadequately. This was awful but he couldn't see what it had to do with her refusing his offer of marriage.

"When she lost the babes my father didn't offer her a word of comfort. When she gave birth, he didn't think to preserve her health by waiting until she'd recovered properly before resuming his visits to her bed. He only ever cared about his pleasure. He never cared about me, his only surviving daughter, either. In his mind, having strapping sons proved his virility as a lover but daughters, and women in general, are useless, only good to be bedded when men need relief." She paused. "That's why I must refuse your offer of marriage."

Magnus blinked. Why would the fact that her father was a despicable individual not worthy of the name prevent her from marrying him? He'd never met the man, would most likely never meet him, so how could it be an issue?

"Forgive me, but I don't understand. What does your parents' sad story have to do with it all?"

Though it was dark, he thought he saw the glint of a tear fall on her cheek. He almost reached out to wipe it.

"I'm scared. I don't want to spend my life like my mother, either with child, or nursing a babe. I don't want to lie in bed for weeks recovering from a difficult birth and dreading the next time my husband comes to my bed to fill my belly with his child. I'm a delicate woman, much more than my mother was, and I don't know how my body could bear it." The sobs she had done her best to keep at bay finally broke through. "It killed her in the end, and I'm very afraid it might kill me too."

The confession tore at Magnus' heart. To think he had accused her of being in love with another man and pleasuring him to win his favor, when the reason for refusing his offer of marriage had been fear. What a boor he really was.

Her pain is my pain Björn had said about the woman he loved. Yes. And now Magnus felt that Agnes' fears were his to soothe.

Without further ado, he swept her into his arms, cradling her against his chest. He couldn't bear to see her cry, but she was right. She was so delicate it was hard to imagine her body going through the ordeal of giving birth time and time again. Her fears were legitimate. Hadn't he thought himself the other day that giving birth was a time fraught with danger for women and that he would hate having to go through what Wolf had gone through with the birth of his second son?

"So you refused me because you don't want to marry at all, not because you didn't want me?" he asked once she had stopped crying.

It had not been personal, she simply thought that remaining an unmarried virgin was the only way not to endanger her health. The relief was overwhelming.

He felt her nod against his chest. "I told you, I want you. But I cannot become your wife, it wouldn't be fair to you. If we marry, you will want children, as any man does, and deserves. Only I can't be the woman giving them to you. So, I have no choice but to refuse your offer, as much as it kills me. 'Tis for the best. One day you will see it." Her face hidden in the crook of his neck, she started sobbing again. "And maybe I will too."

But Magnus knew he would never accept such a thing. If they never married, he would regret it all his life. And so would she. He could not let that happen. Somehow, he needed to find a way to make her see that he wanted her, nothing else. If they never had children, then so be it. He could make his peace with it, as long as she stayed with him to rearrange his tools in odd shapes and wash his back when he helped rescue little girls from burning huts.

He placed her back on the floor and brought his face close to her so she could look him in the eye.

"Sweet. Listen to me. Our marriage doesn't have to be like your parents' was. It will never be like that. We'll make our own way. You're not your mother, and I'm not your father." He gritted his teeth. No, he wasn't like that bastard who thought women were only here to see to his needs. "I don't think women are a vessel for my seed, regardless of the consequences for their health and happiness. I don't expect you to spend half your life carrying or nursing my babies. But there are ways to prevent that."

She stilled. "There are?" She sounded dubious, as if she thought he was only trying to appease her but at least she wasn't crying anymore.

Hate flooded him. Because of her selfish father's behavior, she had no idea that men could be considerate enough to ensure the woman they bedded did not end up with child every time.

"Yes. There are herbs you can take, I believe. And I can withdraw when I reach my pleasure. I've been doing so all my life, as I didn't want to get any of my lovers with child. You can trust me." He placed his forehead against hers. He hated alluding to the other women he had bedded in this moment, but he needed to make her understand that he could control his body to protect hers. "You've seen my seed erupt in your hand. It should prove to you I don't have to be inside you when it happens."

"But... wouldn't you be frustrated?"

Agnes sounded unsure but there was no doubt in his mind. He would not be frustrated. Hell, at the moment he was considering promising never to possess her, just to make her agree never to leave him.

"No. As long as I get to have you in my forge by day, and in my arms at night, I will be the happiest man in the world. I cannot think of any greater honor than calling you my wife and giving you pleasure. Mine doesn't count. It can be achieved in other ways."

She hesitated, as if not daring to admit to a guilty secret. He nodded encouragingly. "I do want children, you know. Just not one every year."

Everything within him tightened, because he'd been prepared to have her as his wife, knowing they would never have any children. But now she was telling him they could be a family one day. His heart almost over-flowed with joy.

"Then it means there will be times when is it safe for me to come inside you, while we try for a babe and while you're already with child." He stopped, not sure he should speak out. His body, not so easily cowed, was urging him on. "In any case, if you really were worried about me getting frustrated, know that your delectable little body can offer me other places to reach my release. I could show you some time, if you wanted."

Heat flared in Agnes's cheeks, because she knew what Magnus meant. "Do you mean my mouth?"

He appeared stunned at her question, as well he might. What had possessed her to mention this? Would he not be appalled at the extent of her knowledge on carnal matters?

"You know about that?" There was something like hope in his voice, when she had expected disgust. It gave her the courage to answer.

"Yes. I saw two people one night in my village, behind the church. The woman was on her knees in front of the man, pleasuring him in that way."

The sight had puzzled her at first. What on earth were the two of them doing? Then the man had let out a moan filled with such lewdness that she had felt hot all the way from her scalp to her toes. She should have walked away at that point, but she had been unable to. Strangely fascinated, she had watched the two lovers until the man had given a grunt and gone stock still, his hands gripping his lover's head with what looked like bruising strength. After a while the woman had stood up laughing, and told him she'd never had to swallow so much in one gulp.

Back home, as she lay on her pallet, Agnes had tried to puzzle out the words. Swallow what exactly? But despite this inexplicable declaration, the idea of taking a man's member in her mouth had intrigued her. She had lacked the courage to do it in the cave when Magnus had agreed to be pleasured, not wanting to shock him in case he didn't know about the practice and thought her depraved. After all, she had never heard it mentioned by anyone and when she had started to stroke him, he had begged her to use her hand, not her mouth. But since he was clearly aware of it, she could not resist asking the question.

"Is that what you meant? That you could reach your release in my mouth?" Now, of course, she knew what the woman had had to swallow. The seed she had seen shoot out of him, the seed that would make her with child if it was released inside her. He was right, this could well be a solution to their problem. Her heart surged in hope. Could a future together be possible?

"Yes." Magnus cleared his throat. "Amongst other things."

It was her turn to be stunned. Other things? What on earth could he mean? Clearly she'd been a fool for thinking herself more experienced than him. Not only did he know all about women taking men into their mouths, but he knew about other deeds she could not even start to suspect. "What do you—"

"Hush, lovely. This is a discussion for another time. Right now, I'm waiting for an answer to my question. The question I asked you in the woods the other day."

She bit the inside of her mouth. "Of course, I want to marry you. How can you doubt it?" Had he not seen by now that her refusal had nothing to do with him?

He hesitated. "Because I was never anyone's first choice. I think I told you about it."

"Yes. You told me your parents always preferred your brother. But surely that's not the same..." Her voice died in her throat when she saw him grimace. This man, tall and confident, as awe-inspiring as a Norse deity, was unsure about his inability to attract a wife?

"It's not all. A few years ago, I bedded a woman from the village called Edith. She was a young widow, and I thought we might come to an understanding. I started to think I should perhaps make her my wife. Then I discovered she was also sharing Sigurd's bed." He paused and swallowed, as if the memory of the discovery caused him pain. "I did not let it deter me. After all, she did not owe me anything at the time and we had never discussed the future. When Sigurd met Frigyth and it became obvious he would not see Edith anymore, I thought I had won and I asked for her hand.

She hesitated at first. Then finally, a few weeks later, she said yes."

Of course she had. A woman had to be mad to refuse such a man's offer. Or mortally scared of the consequences and determined to remain a virgin, like her. Agnes couldn't think of any other reason.

"What happened?"

"I found out that having accepted my offer had not put a stop to her ways. She carried on seducing all the men she thought worthy of interest, and there were many of them, by all accounts. One day, just before our wedding, a Dane called Rune visited the village. She threw herself at him."

"And you saw them together?" She was aghast.

"No. But I heard her tell the woman who had borne Rune's child that she was not sure she wanted to marry me after all. She only kept up the pretense because I was the richest man in the village and she wanted to make the most of that, but she had no intention of being tied down to one man, least of all one who…"

Everything tensed within Agnes. What was he about to reveal? That woman, Edith, sounded awful, but what if her refusal had been motivated by some flaw in Magnus that she, Agnes, had not seen yet? It was possible. Their acquaintance was short.

"One who…" she encouraged, not sure she was ready

to hear what the issue might be. But if they really were to marry, she had to find out now, before it was too late.

"One who was adequate at best in bed."

Adequate?

Everything within Agnes surged at this. She had never slept with Magnus, obviously, but the woman in her, the woman she had tried so hard to suppress over the years, just knew he would be more than adequate as a lover. He would be selfless, indefatigable, passionate.

How could anyone, himself included, doubt it?

"Oh, Magnus, I'm so sorry. It will have been awful for you to hear all this."

He nodded. "It was. So when I heard that you had been supposed to marry Björn, I assumed this was why you had refused me. Because all the while you had been hankering after someone else and were waiting for a better offer, from someone you—"

"No! Never!" she exploded. "I'm sorry for hurting you, it was never my intention. I should have told you why I was refusing you. But I thought you could not possibly be interested in me and had only proposed because you felt guilty about what had happened in the cave, and by the tub."

"No, even if I do feel guilty for it." He made a grimace then drew her close to him. "But I proposed because it did not take me long to understand that I cannot live without you. And what do you mean, I couldn't possibly be interested in you?"

She lowered her gaze to the floor. "I'm shy." Wouldn't he prefer a more assertive woman for a wife, someone his own age?

"You're not shy, really. Not with me, at least." A glance at her hand made his meaning clear. She had not hesitated in pleasuring him when he'd asked. "And even if you were, why would it be a problem?"

She had no answer to that. It wasn't a problem, exactly, and if he didn't object, then why should she? "We are near strangers."

"Strangers who have lived and slept together for days, who have shared intimacies usually reserved to lovers. Strangers who understand one another."

"But I'm a Saxon. I don't know anything about your culture."

He gave a slanted smile. "No one knows this, but for years I've been envious of Wolf, Sigurd and Rune, and now Björn, for getting a Saxon wife. Now I won't have to be. I will have my own beautiful Saxon at home."

Everything inside her melted at the declaration. Then she forced herself to focus. "I'm so tiny compared to you."

He growled. "Ah, now, this is actually one of my

favorite things about you. Because it means I can do this."

Before she could wonder what he meant, he lifted her into his arms, forcing her to wrap her legs around his waist. "If you weighed the same as me, you infuriating, shy Saxon woman, I could not pin you to the wall to take you like the wild Norseman I am, now could I? And it's something I have been dreaming of doing ever since you arrived in the village."

"You wanted to p-pin me to the wall?" She could barely breathe for the sheer intensity of the moment. Magnus felt so strong between her thighs, so warm, and so, well, *wild*.

"Yes." With her still wrapped around him, he walked over to the window and trapped her between the wall and his hard body. "I wanted to slide into you until you couldn't think of anything other than me, deep inside you, filling you to the hilt. I still do."

Well, he had her pinned to the wall now, didn't he? So what was he waiting for? They had just agreed to get married, and she knew he would give her time to prepare before he made her with child. It was safe. She could at last find out what men and women did together.

"Do it now. Take me," she breathed, scarcely crediting her boldness. Perhaps he had a point. With him she wasn't exactly shy.

He groaned but didn't move. "No. Not like this. You're a virgin, and I should—"

"I won't break, Magnus. Take me, here, now, like this, up against the wall, the way you wanted to, while you still want me."

His nostrils flared. "I'll always want you."

"Then prove it."

A heartbeat later she felt him shift and lift her skirts so he could rub his steel length against her soft folds. Oh Lord, he was so hard, so ready, and she so desperate that she could not help but grind her hips in search of the friction she needed.

"Look at me, my love," he grunted, tightening his hold around her. "I'll have you look at me when I make you mine."

"I'm already yours."

"And I yours. But I need to see I'm not hurting you. Well, not unbearably so, at least," he amended in a bid at honesty. "I would give ten years of my life to be the one enduring the pain of our first joining."

"And I would not have it for the world, for I mean to have you by my side for as long as possible." She threw him what she hoped was a scorching look. Judging from the way his eyes caught ablaze, she had done a fair job of it. "Please, Magnus, take me."

Finally, he relented. Holding her up with one arm,

he quickly freed his erection and then positioned himself at her entrance. Suddenly she didn't mind being tiny, since it meant he could use her in that delicious manner. It was unbearably arousing to be at the mercy of her fiery lover. She expected him to plunge inside in one thrust but he spoke instead.

"Bare your breasts to me. I need to suckle you, make you wet for me."

"I... I already am." Well, if felt more as if the place between her thighs had swollen to twice its size, but she imagined that was what he meant. It was certainly throbbing, calling out to him.

He ignored her answer. "Lower your bodice, Agnes, or there will not be anything left of your dress to salvage. This is for me was well as for you. I *need* to suckle your perfect breasts. The memory of them has been driving me mad for days."

She did as she was ordered.

A heartbeat later, a warm mouth engulfed her nipple. She squirmed, not knowing if she wanted to escape the searing heat or force him to suckle her harder. He held her ruthlessly in place while he feasted on her. Just when she thought she could not take it any longer, he surged upward, breaching her entrance. Agnes cried out. She had no idea if he'd sheathed his whole length inside her but it certainly felt like it.

He paused and slid in a fraction more, answering her question, and then he stilled, giving her time to absorb the new sensations.

"All right?" he rasped.

"Yes. Are you all right?" It had to be killing him not to move.

He gave something like a chuckle. "I will be in a moment, when I feel you relax around me. Breathe, lovely."

She did, and as he'd foreseen, her body relaxed, allowing him to slide in a bit further. Oh, so she'd been mistaken to think he'd buried himself to the hilt. How much more was there to take? She already felt impossibly stretched.

"So good," he breathed. "So perfect for me."

The words he said between his teeth next were probably the filthiest she had ever heard, and they only inflamed her further. "Yes," she moaned, now knowing what she was agreeing to. It didn't seem to matter.

"I will not stop until you've come," he said, his voice as gruff as if he'd issued a warning, when it was the most wonderful promise she had ever heard.

Slowly, he began pounding in earnest, holding her against the wall, legs spread wide. In that position, she could do nothing but take what he wanted to give her, at the speed he wanted to give it. And soon she understood that it was exactly what she needed.

She cried out when heat flooded her, dissolving everything in its path.

"Oh, Magnus, you've stolen my bones!"

This had to be the most ridiculous thing she, or anyone, had ever said but he didn't laugh. Instead, he buried his face into her neck and bit her. It was gentle, but it was unmistakably a bite. The spasms he'd created between her legs, which had started to ebb, started anew.

She barely registered when he walked over to the pallet in the other room with his shaft still embedded deep within her. "My turn," he said darkly, sliding one hand under her left knee to open her wider for his possession.

"Yes."

Agnes had meant to watch him take his pleasure, knowing she would enjoy the sight of him poised over but she had not counted on the fact that feeling him surging inside her again and again would stir her desire anew, and she was unable to hold on to her resolve to watch him. Her head rolled back and her eyes closed of their own accord.

She whimpered and all too soon the overwhelming sensations she'd felt earlier flooded her, starting at the place where they were joined and radiating all through her body.

"Yes," Magnus growled. "You again. Now me. Please, sweetheart, steal my bones. They're yours anyway, as is every part of me."

True to his promise, at the last moment, he withdrew and fisted his shaft, which seemed to have grown to inhumane proportions while inside her. The guttural cry he gave when he spurted like he had that day in the cave caused her insides to convulse. White splashes fell onto her stomach, deliciously warm and sticky. It was the most beautiful thing Agnes had ever seen, because it was the proof of his understanding and readiness to offer her the life she had always thought would be denied to her. It was the proof that she could have the choice over what was done to her body and he would respect it, no matter how strong his need for release.

Lost to the joy of the moment, she had forgotten all about the risks linked to their lovemaking. He had not. He had honored his word, at the cost of a great personal sacrifice, and made sure she didn't have to face the consequences of her decision to marry before she was ready to do so. It was the best proof of love she had ever have received. Magnus hadn't lied.

He wanted *her*, not just the pleasure her body could offer him.

Slowly, her gaze locked with his, she trailed a finger in the pearly substance coating her skin and swallowed back tears of gratitude.

"I love you, Magnus. One day soon, I promise, I will bear your children, the children you deserve. In the meantime, I will give you everything I have."

"Everything?" He sounded out of breath, which was little wonder, considering what he'd been doing. By rights he should be unable to move. "Love, I would be happy with only half that."

Her lips wobbled. How could she not love that man? "Be sure to remember it when I rail at you in anger, or make you do something you don't want to do."

He placed his forehead against hers in a tender, loving gesture. "Mm. This is what marriage is all about, I believe. I can't wait."

They remained side by side a long moment. Then Magnus placed a kiss on her temple. The gesture was so tender that it brought a tear to her eyes. Where was the wild lover who had pinned her to the wall only moments ago?

"Do you know what this village has never seen?" She shook her head, too spent to answer. "Two weddings in two days. I think things are about to change."

Her chest exploded. "You mean—"

"I do. So get some sleep, sweetheart, for tomorrow, I wed you."

"Magnus, you have to let me get up now, or we will miss the wedding," Agnes gasped when her husband's big, warm hand landed over her naked breast.

He'd just rolled off her sated body but apparently, he was ready for more. It did not surprise her. Not only was the man insatiable, but he was also generous, and he liked nothing more than to use his mouth on her while she was recovering from his lovemaking. Usually she loved it but today they had to get ready, or they would not reach the village in time.

Magnus groaned. "Bloody Sven. Always finding new ways to upset me. Getting married of all things, and on the day I want nothing more than to spend time in bed with my wife before getting up."

Agnes let out a pearly laugh. "Now, be fair. He would have been hard pressed to choose a day when you *didn't* want to do that. It's what you seem to want to do most days." She should know, she who benefitted from it.

"Mm. Yes, I said. Bloody Sven." He gave her breast a squeeze, not in the least chastened. "Why did he have to get married at all is what I want to know. I'm not sure if I should pity the poor woman who agreed to have him or question her sanity."

"Ella seems perfectly lovely," Agnes said with a smile. "This marriage will be the making of him, I think."

A snort was all she got in answer, but in truth, the relationship between the two brothers had improved immensely since she and Magnus had gotten married. Her husband seemed to have found a new, inner strength that allowed him to withstand his brother's attacks with more patience. And now that he was getting married also, Sven might put a stop to his petty teasing. Agnes dearly hoped so, for it always hurt her to see Magnus in pain.

The hand at her breast became more insistent and Agnes could feel herself yielding to the silent demand.

"Please, Magnus. I'm trying to be sensible and do the right thing," she pleaded. She had always found it hard to resist his entreaties and her body had already started to melt. Soon it would be too late. She would be the one pouncing on him. "I know you don't want to miss the wedding, really."

"You're right, as always." He sighed and drew her on top of him. The ease with which he moved her about never failed to arouse her. In his arms she never wished to be taller or anything other than what she was. They were just perfect together. "At least give me one last kiss before we go, wife."

The "last" kiss was as scorching as a prelude to wild lovemaking would have been, and left Agnes sightly breathless.

"I will prepare something to eat while you get the cart ready," she offered, before she could let herself be swayed.

"Yes. That will be for the best."

After a one last tap on her naked buttocks, Magnus jumped to his feet.

Cursing Sven under her breath for getting married today of all days, when she wanted nothing more than to stay in bed with her husband, Agnes hastily got dressed. Then she gathered some cheese, a few nuts and a loaf of bread in a square of cloth, grabbed a wineskin filled with ale, and joined her husband by the stable.

Moments later they were on their way. Draped in a thick wolf's pelt that made his shoulders appear twice as wide as usual, Magnus was magnificent. She already knew she would enjoy removing it when she dragged him to whatever quiet corner she could find to finish what they had started this morning.

"I might be tempted to stop by the cave, you know, when we make our way back from the wedding," he told her with a wink as they entered the forest.

Had he read her mind? Probably, as she wouldn't be surprised if the desire she felt for him was etched all over her face. But the cave was the worst idea he had ever had. Despite the heat in her body, Agnes shivered.

"The one with the bats? Forgive me, but I'm not tempted."

Magnus threw her a scorching look. "I have fond memories of that day, you know."

She did know it. He often alluded to what she had done to him that day. "If that's what you want, I can do that anytime, anywhere. Just, please, let's not go in that cave."

"Anytime, anywhere? I will hold you to that promise, dear wife."

She smiled and placed a hand over his strong thigh, high enough to make him tense up in anticipation. No,

Agnes was definitely not shy anymore. The little flame she'd been had become a scorching brazier, burning bright and strong.

"I hope so, my wild Norseman."

ABOUT THE AUTHOR

As far back as I remember, I have been attracted to the Middle Ages, to knights in shining armour and their ladies in spectacular dresses. Now I get to write about them, I feel like the luckiest woman in the world. Being French and married to a Brit makes each book I write extra special, as our countries share a long and sometimes painful past. But in the end, in life as well as in fiction, love conquers all!

I have published several medieval romances under my own name, including series, and also have a pen name, Judith Falcon, for spicier projects, still in historical romance.

Join my newsletter and check out my other books on virginiemarconato.com.

ALSO BY VIRGINIE MARCONATO

The Noble Norsemen

Taming the Wolf

Soothing the Beast

Wooing the Devil

Baiting the Bear

Tempting the Saxon

Seducing the Warrior

Loving the Blacksmith

www.ingramcontent.com/pod-product-compliance
Lightning Source LLC
Chambersburg PA
CBHW050405110726
47899CB00008B/2664